Second-hand Family

Richard Parker

Second-hand Family

Illustrated by Gareth Floyd

THE CHILDREN'S BOOK CLUB
121 CHARING CROSS ROAD
LONDON W.C.2

By the same author NEW HOME SOUTH
THE HOUSE THAT GUILDA DREW
THE BOY WHO WASN'T LONELY

This edition by arrangement with
Brockhampton Press Ltd

First edition 1965
Text copyright © 1965 Richard Parker
Illustrations copyright © 1965 Brockhampton Press Ltd
Printed in Great Britain by
Richard Clay (The Chaucer Press) Ltd, Bungay, Suffolk

Contents

Contents

1 No. 73

Giles Willis did not often get the chance to ride in a car, so it was a pity Mr Judd's car had to be so horrid. The inside smelt strongly of stale cigarette smoke and the stuff Mr Judd put on his hair.

Giles fiddled with the handle that moved the window up and down. 'Do you mind if I open the window a bit?' he asked.

'And let all that cold air in?' said Mr Judd. 'You're joking!'

Giles sighed quietly and decided that if he breathed gently through his mouth the smell would not seem so bad. He glanced over his shoulder to make sure that his suitcase was on the back seat where he had put it, and then peered forward through the slightly steamy wind-screen at the other cars on the road. A Zodiac, a Cortina, a Vauxhall Victor, and a red Austin Mini flicked past. Then an old black Citroën.

'That's a French car,' Giles said.

'What?'

'A French car.'

Mr Judd turned his head miles too late to see it.

'Oh,' he said. Then they were silent for a while.

They came out of the thirty-mile limit into something that was almost country. There were low fields on either side, some of them flooded. A narrow stream half-blocked with reeds ran round one of the fields, and there were five swans in the water. Two of the swans were white and the other three pale grey, as if they had been playing in a dusty shed and not yet cleaned themselves up. Giles guessed that the grey ones must be half-grown cygnets that had hatched out that last summer; he was going to say something about them to Mr Judd, but decided not to, as Mr Judd would almost certainly say 'What?' and be too late to see them.

Giles saw nothing of interest for the next mile or so and then there were three huge yellow machines on a slope to the left of the road. One of them was tearing up tree roots and the other two were shoving tons of earth about, making the slope into flat land.

Mr Judd cleared his throat and said suddenly and rather loudly, 'The house I'm taking you to, Giles, is in the next village. Only a couple of miles now.'

'Oh,' said Giles.

'The people's name is Maxwell.'

Giles shrugged his shoulders slightly.

'You don't sound very interested.'

Giles shrugged again.

'Well, surely,' said Mr Judd, his voice going a little squeaky with annoyance, 'Well, surely, you'd rather live with foster-parents than in the Home, wouldn't you?'

8

'Oh, it's not bad in the Home,' said Giles truthfully.

'But better with foster-parents!'

'Sometimes,' said Giles. He had lived with two different families in the last year. 'It all depends. You can't help feeling in the way and . . . oh, I don't know. It doesn't matter much anyway. If you haven't got a family of your own, it doesn't matter where you go.'

'You mustn't feel like that,' said Mr Judd. 'We try very hard to find the right sort of foster-parents for each of you. Now this Maxwell family . . .'

He went on talking, slowly and precisely, and now and then glancing at Giles to see if he was listening. Giles pretended he was, but in fact he had gone off into a dream of his own. Once he did have a family of his own. He could only just remember. He blinked hard, shook his head and looked out of the window. What was the good of thinking like that? He had to put up with things the way they were.

'What's this place?' he said, interrupting Mr Judd without knowing it.

'Haleshangar,' Mr Judd said. 'It's the village I've been telling you about. Where the Maxwells live.'

'Not much like a village. It's beastly. Look at those great black heaps over there!'

On the right of the road, stretching as far as you could see, was a great high hill, almost a mountain, of greyish black, with nothing at all growing on it. In places there were hideous green or yellow patches and streaks, as if the heap had gone mouldy. In front of the mountain were dirty buildings, rusty machinery, and two huge wheels at the top of a wooden tower.

9

'That's the pit head,' said Mr Judd. 'And the heap is the dust and rubbish they get out of the coal. Haleshangar is a mining village, you see. We turn off here.'

He swung the car down a turning to the left. On either side of the road were houses and more houses all exactly alike. They all looked shabby and much in need of a coat of paint. On either side there were other turnings, with even more of the same houses going on for ever.

Giles shuddered. What a dreadful place to live, he thought. He opened his mouth to say something about it to Mr Judd, then changed his mind and closed his mouth again. The car came to a stop in front of one of the houses. It was just like all the others except that it had the number 73 on the front gate-post.

'Well,' said Mr Judd. 'Come on!'

Giles started to get out of the car.

'Bring your bag, then.'

Giles went back to the car and got his bag. As he felt the weight of it he had a horrible feeling of depression. He suddenly realized that he really was going to be left with this quite strange family that he had never seen before. Just left, like a parcel on someone's doorstep, or like an old unwanted bedstead being dumped in a wood. His feet seemed rooted into the pavement as he watched Mr Judd go down the front path and knock on the front door of number 73. Mr Judd turned then and saw that Giles had not followed him.

'Giles!' he said sharply, and made a little sign with his hand to tell Giles to come quickly.

Giles uprooted his feet and trudged through the gateway and along the narrow path. He was just behind Mr Judd when the door opened. The door did not open wide in a welcoming sort of way; just a few inches, enough to show half the face and head of a girl of about twelve; Giles' own age. She had short, fair hair and her face had such an unpleasant scowl of suspicion, that it was not possible to say immediately whether she was good-looking or not.

'What do you want?' she demanded, and darted quick glances at Mr Judd, at Giles, at his bag and then at the car standing near the kerb. 'You're not the insurance, are you?'

'No,' said Mr Judd. 'I'm not the insurance.' He seemed to find this question rather funny. 'But you're Linda Maxwell, aren't you?'

'What if I am?' said the girl, not at all pleased that Mr Judd knew her name.

'This is Giles Willis,' said Mr Judd, nodding down at Giles and his suitcase. 'You've heard about him, haven't you? I've brought him to live with you. I'm sure you two will be great friends.'

Linda looked at Giles as if she did not think this very likely. 'It's nothing to do with me,' she said. 'Mum fixed it all up. She's down the shop.'

'Never mind,' said Mr Judd. 'We'll just sit down and wait for her. I don't suppose she'll be very long.'

He moved forward as if he thought the girl would step back and open the door to him, but instead she pushed it nearly shut until all that could be seen of her was one eye and her rather sharp nose.

11

'I can't let you in,' she said. 'You'll have to wait out there until she comes. She doesn't like me to let anyone in when I'm here by myself.'

'Very sensible, I'm sure,' said Mr Judd, although Giles guessed from his voice that he was annoyed. 'We'll wait in the car until your mother comes. I don't suppose she'll be long.'

'You don't know Mum when she gets down the shop,' said Linda. 'Talks for hours sometimes.' And with that she shut the door completely.

Mr Judd and Giles went back to the car. Mr Judd sat inside, but Giles preferred to sit on his case on the pavement. Mr Judd smoked a cigarette and looked at his watch every minute or so. After about ten minutes he threw the stub away and got out again.

'You wait here,' he told Giles. 'I'll just go along to the shop and see if I can hurry Mrs Maxwell up a little.'

'All right,' said Giles. He didn't think much of the idea, but he couldn't think of anything better.

He watched Mr Judd walk down the street and disappear round the first corner. Then he waited, sitting on the suitcase, for what seemed like hours and nothing at all happened. Once he caught sight of Linda staring at him from an upstairs window. Immediately she saw him looking she put her tongue out and then disappeared.

At one point three little boys playing in the street came and stood in a row in front of Giles and stared at him. 'What are you doing here?' one of them said.

'Cooking myself some bacon and eggs,' said Giles.

They went on staring at him without smiling.

'Doing what?' said the one who had spoken before.

'I'm waiting for a train,' said Giles.

The three little boys looked carefully up and down the street as if looking to see whether the train was coming. 'Will it come down this road then?' one of them asked.

'Of course it will.'

'Where you going to, then?'

'Margate,' said Giles. 'Want to come?'

'Coo,' they said.

'Have to ask your mums first, won't you?'

The three little boys looked at each other and then ran off in different directions, making excited squeaky noises. One of them lived quite near; after a few minutes a woman came to the gate and stared at Giles.

'That's him,' said the little boy, pointing.

'Don't be so daft,' said the woman, and aiming a swipe at the boy's head with her open hand, went back into the house again.

Giles tapped a tune on the side of his case and hummed to himself, pretending to be more cheerful than he felt. A tall, thin boy of about eighteen came slouching down the road towards him. He had dark hair, straight and so long that it hung right over his jacket collar and almost covered his ears. His trousers were black, and so tight on his legs that they gave him a spidery look. Giles stopped humming; he couldn't help staring at this boy.

When the boy came level with Giles he walked a complete circle round the car, tapping the windows, the front wings, the headlights with his knuckles as he went. When he got round to Giles again he stopped and stared at him for a few seconds as if he was some odd creature washed up by the tide, then he turned abruptly away and went up the path to number 73. He gave the knocker three good bangs, rang the bell twice and then disappeared round the side of the house before anyone could answer.

Giles watched with interest to see what would happen. Nothing did for a few minutes, and then the door opened cautiously and part of Linda's face could be seen peering through the crack. The door opened a little wider, then it came right open and Linda came out on to the step. She looked all round, thoroughly mystified until she saw Giles still sitting on his case out in the street.

'Was that you?' she said. Giles shook his head.

14

'Did you see who it was, then?' she asked sharply.

'A big boy. He had tight black trousers on and hair long like a girl.'

'Oh,' said Linda. She put her head back inside the door and called out, 'That you, Martin?'

Giles heard a laugh from somewhere inside the house.

'I suppose you think that's funny,' shouted Linda.

This time there was no answer. Linda came slowly down the path and leaned on the gate, swinging it open and shut with her elbows and looking at Giles.

'Are you really going to live here?' she asked.

'That's what Mr Judd told me.'

'Where's he gone?'

'Down the shop to find your mum.'

Linda considered this for a while, then she said, 'I suppose if you're going to live here anyway you might as well come in.'

'I don't mind waiting,' Giles said.

Even so he picked up his bag and followed Linda into the house, looking about him curiously as he went. Well, he thought as he stood in the small hallway, this is it. This is your new home.

'Wipe your shoes on the mat then!' said Linda in a scolding voice. 'Didn't they ever teach you anything where you come from?'

Giles meekly did as he was told, wondering at the same time what Mrs Maxwell would be like; like Linda, only worse probably.

2 *Plenty of difficulties*

When Giles followed Linda through into the sitting-room, he was rather surprised. It did not look much like the sort of house where people worried about wiping their shoes. In the first place he had never seen anywhere so untidy. Papers and gramophone records, shoes and bits of clothing were lying about all over the place. There was a cup and saucer underneath one of the armchairs, the cup on its side and a small pool of tea dried on the lino like a circle of wrinkled brown skin.

There was a table pushed against the wall under the window. On the front half of it was a sewing-machine, but on the back half were what looked like the breakfast things, still not cleared away, although it was the middle of the morning. But Giles only glanced at these things, for something much more interesting was going on. The sewing-machine was whirring away and a man in shirt-sleeves and braces was sitting up to it feeding pieces of bright red material into it.

Giles thought only women used sewing-machines, so he watched fascinated. The man was very thin and pale. His hands seemed to be made of cords and bones. He had thin, fluffy, pale brown hair which just at that moment was damp and stuck to his forehead. His face was very wide at the top, his eyes sunk deep in his head, like shy brown creatures peeping out of their burrows under the roots of a tree. His chin was narrow and pointed. The pinkish-grey colour of his skin and the hollow look of his cheeks made the man look ill or half-starved.

Linda sat in one of the armchairs, curled her feet up out of sight and started reading a magazine which had on the cover a picture of a boy with his mouth open as if he was shouting and holding a guitar in front of him. She did not take any further interest in Giles.

The man at the sewing-machine went on working for some time. Every now and then he shot quick glances at Giles as if wondering how he had got there. Giles was not at all sure what to do, so he simply stood still where he was with his suitcase in his hand.

After a few minutes the machine stopped its whirring abruptly. The man lifted the needle, cut the thread with his teeth and then turned right round to have a good look at Giles.

'Who are you, then?' he asked. His voice wasn't either friendly or unfriendly. It was quiet and breathy, something like wind blowing through stiff rushes.

'Giles Willis,' said Giles.

'Giles Willis, eh?' The man nodded. A quick, birdlike nod. Then he caught sight of Giles' suitcase. 'Oh,' he said, 'you'd be from the . . . I mean you're the lad who they . . .'

17

'Mr Judd brought me in his car,' Giles said shyly.

'Mr Judd?' said the man, and by this time Giles had guessed that he must be Linda's father, Mr Maxwell. 'Oh I see. You mean . . .'

The rest of the sentence was lost under a great roar of noise that came from somewhere upstairs. It sounded as if half a dozen giants were shouting at the tops of their voices and at the same time a couple o circus bands were trying to make enough noise to drown them. It was hard to make out the words but they sounded like:

> Crazy 'bout loving,
> Yea, yea.
> Crazy like crazy,
> Yea, yea, yea.
> Loving like crazy,
> And I know, and I know, and I know.
> Yea.
> AND I KNOW!

Mr Maxwell raised his eyes towards the ceiling. The corners of his mouth turned down almost as if he was going to start crying. Then he shrugged his shoulders and turned back to the machine.

Giles decided that the noise must be a record-player turned up very loud and that Martin must be the one who was playing it. Mr Maxwell had obviously given up any idea of going on with what he had been saying, so Giles put his case down again and sat on it, waiting for something else to happen.

After a minute or so the record came to an end.

There was a strange hush. Mr Maxwell looked at Giles. 'What I mean . . .' he began to say.

But that was all he had time for. The music from upstairs burst out again—

> Crazy 'bout loving,
> Yea, yea . . .

When it stopped a second time, neither Giles nor Mr Maxwell tried to say anything. They just sat and waited for it to begin again. And it did.

However, part way through the third playing of the record there were sounds in the hall of a door slamming and a woman's voice being raised.

'Martin! Turn that thing down! Do you hear me? If you don't turn it down this minute I'll come up and throw it out of the window!'

This sounded very interesting. Giles got up off his suitcase wondering what would happen. The noise ceased altogether and there was dead silence.

After a few seconds the woman's voice came again, quite loud still, but not shouting. 'There! That's better. So sorry, Mr Judd. Do come in, won't you?'

The door opened and Mr Judd and Mrs Maxwell came in. Mr Maxwell at the machine went on working until he had finished his seam, then he turned sideways in his chair, nodded at Giles as if to say, 'Now we'll soon know what's what,' and fixed his eyes steadily on his wife.

Mrs Maxwell was a tall woman. Her hair was short, black and glossy. She was very good-looking. She smiled at Giles as if she knew him and was pleased to see him again. One of her top front teeth was partly filled with gold, and this, together with the dark hair, and the graceful way Mrs Maxwell moved, made Giles think for a moment of gipsies. At the same time he felt, for the first time that day, that living with the Maxwells might not be so bad after all. He smiled back at her and would have said something, but she had already turned away to speak to Mr Judd and he was too late.

'You can be sure the poor lad will have a proper home with us, Mr Judd,' Mrs Maxwell was saying. Giles did not much like being called a 'poor lad', but he did not interrupt.

'I'm sure . . .' said Mr Judd.

Mrs Maxwell's voice swept over him like the tide over flat sand. 'But I do want one thing to be clearly understood,' she said, sinking gracefully back into an

armchair and flinging one arm out as if she was speaking to a large audience rather than just the one man. 'Yes, as I said in my letter, I simply can't guarantee to keep him anything over six months. You see, it does so much depend on . . . well, other things. To be frank the money will come in very handy. Especially just at the moment. Doug – that's Mr Maxwell here – has had a long illness, as you know, and things have been very difficult for all of us. Behind with some of our payments for a start . . .'

'Now Barbara!' said Mr Maxwell quietly. 'Mr Judd doesn't want to hear . . .'

'He wants to know the facts,' cried Mrs Maxwell. 'Of course he does. I'll look after the boy like a second mother, that I do promise. But I'm not going to pretend. We need the money, and that's a fact.'

Giles did not feel he could stay a moment longer and hear himself being talked about in this way. He got up and quickly left the room. As he only knew his way through the front door, that was the way he went, and found himself alone a few seconds later, standing out in the street. After a moment's hesitation he thrust both hands into his trouser pockets and began to walk away from the main road, not looking particularly where he was going, but frowning at the pavement a yard or so in front of his moving feet.

So it was going to be the same old thing over again. People just put up with him, for two or three months, in order to get whatever money it was Mr Judd brought around for them every week. It was never him they wanted. No one had ever wanted Giles Willis. As far as they were concerned it could have been any of the boys from the Home.

After the way Mrs Maxwell had smiled at him, Giles had had a sudden notion that she might have been passing the Home and glancing over the fence of the playground seen him – Giles – and stopped and said, 'There's a nice-looking boy; just the sort of son I should have liked to have. I'll adopt him, that's what I'll do.'

Instead of these words, Giles could now hear ringing in his head others not at all like them. 'We need the money, and that's a fact.'

He pushed his hands so far down in his pockets that his shoulders became hunched. He strode on, not noticing the street he walked through, the houses on each side or the occasional people he passed. What did it matter, anyway? You didn't have to have a family. It was all right being on your own, really. Families weren't all that good. They were always arguing and fighting. He wouldn't want to be adopted by the Maxwells, not even if they asked him. That snooty Linda, and Martin with his noisy record-player, and Mr Maxwell doing a woman's job and looking like a washed-out duster . . .

Yet somehow, as he thought of Mr Maxwell, he had an odd feeling, as if he was sorry for him. But that was no good. You ought not to feel sorry for your father. That wasn't what fathers were for. No, the Maxwells were no good.

Having come to that conclusion, Giles felt a bit better. He walked on for a while without thinking of anything, and gradually the walking seemed to relax him. He felt he might as well go back. He didn't want to make a fuss. He didn't want them to come out looking for him.

As this thought came to him he reached the end of the pavement and stopped dead in his tracks. He raised his eyes and discovered that he had reached the end of the street and the end of the village. It stopped as if it had been cut through with an axe. Behind him was the concrete street and the rows and rows of houses all exactly alike; in front of him was a muddy cart-track cutting across a ploughed field. The land sloped away, and in the dip was a large red farm-house surrounded by barns and dairies and stables. Beyond that again were more fields and eventually a large wood which stretched as far as he could see up the distant slope. He saw pigeons flying up out of the corner of the wood, swing out in the empty air and throw themselves back like stones into the trees. He saw a hundred or so black-headed gulls moiling up and down behind a tractor. He was watching them fascinated when he heard hurried steps behind him and turned to see who it was. He was relieved to see it was only Linda.

She came to a stop a couple of yards from him, too puffed to speak for a moment.

'What's the matter?' he said. 'House on fire or something?'

'Course not.'

'You were running.'

'I can run if I like, I suppose.'

23

Giles laughed. 'Sorry,' he said. 'And I suppose I can go for a walk if I like.'

Linda had been looking at him with a cross expression on her face. Now she was embarrassed and looked away, over Giles' shoulder and down towards the farm. 'Nice over there in the summer,' she said. 'Too muddy now. But we go over that way sometimes when it's a bit drier.'

Giles turned round and they both looked at the seagulls. Giles knew without asking that Linda did not want to say anything about being sent out to look for him. After a couple of minutes of standing side by side and saying nothing, Giles said, 'Better be getting back, then.'

'I suppose so,' said Linda.

'Has Mr Judd gone?'

'Don't know.'

They walked slowly, side by side, back the way Giles had come. 'You won't like living with us,' Linda said suddenly, the way people say things they have been thinking some time until they can hardly bear to get the words out. 'We're a horrible sort of family really.'

Giles was shocked. 'You ought not to say that,' he objected. 'I mean, your own family . . .'

'What do you know about families?'

'Not much,' Giles admitted. 'All the same . . . I thought your dad was nice.'

Linda did not answer for a moment. Then she said, 'He's always being ill.'

'He can't help that, can he?'

24

'Course not. But it's pretty miserable for us when he is. Oh, and Martin never keeps a proper job, and that makes rows. And Mum is too slapdash and untidy, and ... but I expect you'll find all that out for yourself.'

Giles thought it was best not to answer this at all. He did not like to hear Linda running her own family down. They went quite a way in silence, almost to the gate of number 73. Then Linda gave a wicked little chuckle and said to him:

'I'll tell you one thing you're not going to like one little bit; you're going to have to sleep with Martin. We've only got two proper bedrooms. I sleep in a tiny room about the size of a coffin. Still, Martin's bed is quite a big one.'

'I shan't mind that,' said Giles, determined not to be put off by difficulties.

Linda swung the gate open and grinned at him over her shoulder. 'Wait till you hear what Martin has to say about it. He's been going off the deep end ever since Mum said we were going to take someone in. First it was going to be a lodger, but that meant buying another bed. So then Mum decided to have someone like you, and Martin said if she did he'd get a job somewhere away from home, and Mum said the day Martin got a job we'd all hang the flags out, and that's how it ended up.'

'Oh!' said Giles. He seemed to be having plenty of difficulties for his first day.

3 Nice brother Martin

When Giles and Linda got back indoors, the first thing Giles noticed was the odd expressions on the faces of Mr Judd and Mrs Maxwell. If they'd been children he would have said they had done something wrong and were afraid of being found out. As they were grown ups Giles guessed they must have been talking about him and were hoping he had not heard whatever it was they had been saying. They needn't have worried; he hadn't heard a thing.

'Oh, there you are, Linda,' Mrs Maxwell said. 'Look, why don't you show Giles where he'll be sleeping, and where the bathroom is and . . . all that?'

'Come on!' said Linda. 'Bring your case, silly!' she added sharply when Giles stepped over it.

'Linda!' said Mrs Maxwell.

From half-way up the stairs Giles heard Mr Maxwell say, 'Much better to take no notice, dear. It's bound to take a week or so for them to get used to each other. After that they'll be the best of friends. You'll see.'

Linda made a loud snorting noise. 'Aren't parents

corny!' she exclaimed. 'As if we were puppies or something.'

Giles shrugged his shoulders. 'Grown-ups just like to talk,' he said. 'You don't have to listen.'

At the top of the stairs Linda stopped so suddenly that Giles thumped her in the back of the knees with the edge of the case. 'Sorry,' he said.

Linda did not seem to notice. She was scowling at some idea she'd had. 'Do you think we'll be the best of friends?' she asked aggressively.

'Hadn't thought about it.'

'Well, don't count on it. I like to choose my own friends.'

'I expect I'll manage,' said Giles.

'Good. As long as we've got that clear. Now come into the lion's den and be eaten alive.' She turned to the first door at the top of the stairs and knocked loudly.

'Go away!' shouted a voice from inside.

'Nice brother I've got,' said Linda. She turned the handle, but the door was locked.

'Open up, Martin,' she shouted. 'Mum told me to show Giles up. You've got to unlock it.'

'Drop dead.'

Linda rattled the handle. 'I'll count ten and then I'll go and tell Mum.'

There was a groan from inside and a few seconds later the sound of a key turning in the lock. Linda opened the door, but Martin was standing just inside barring the way.

'No need for you both to come in,' he said.

27

Linda drew back immediately. 'Don't think I want to come into your smelly room,' she said and sniffed at the cigarette smoke that was swirling about. 'I don't know where you get the money from to buy cigarettes. You haven't had a job for months.'

'I steal them,' said Martin, making a hideous face. 'Didn't you guess?'

'Don't say such things,' said Linda, 'or I'll . . .'

'I'll tell Mum!' said Martin in a squeaky voice that was supposed to sound like Linda.

Linda was too cross to speak. She turned and ran down the stairs. Martin leaned over the banisters to laugh at her, then he went back into his room saying over his shoulder, 'You'd better come in then.'

Giles carried his bag into the bedroom, put it down just inside the door and looked round. Martin leapt from half-way across the room and dived on to the double bed that was pulled close under the window. Once there he rolled over on his back and sprawled from corner to corner with his hands behind his head and stared at Giles.

'Well?' he said.

'It's a very nice room,' Giles said politely. Actually it was rather untidy with shirts and odds and ends of clothing hanging on the backs of chairs and dangling from half-open drawers. The walls were almost smothered with large coloured pictures torn from magazines. As far as Giles could see they were of various pop singers.

Although it was a good-sized room, there wasn't much space in it for moving about in. A set of drums

filled up one corner, and half of one wall was occupied with a stack of black boxes, panels with switches and loud-speakers. Wires wriggled about the floor like thin black snakes. There was a guitar on the top of the wardrobe and another on the chest of drawers. There didn't seem anywhere in the room where Giles could sit down. In fact as he stood by the door he seemed to be in the only empty space there was.

'Shut the door,' Martin said from the bed. 'And turn the key.'

Giles was about to do this when the door opened suddenly in his face and Linda's head poked through.

'Not you again,' said Martin.

Linda said, 'Mum says you're to empty one of the drawers in the chest for Giles.'

'Oh, she does, does she?'

'Yes,' said Linda. 'So you'd better do it.' She shut the door again quickly before Martin could say anything more.

Martin climbed slowly off the bed and went to the chest as if he was wading through treacle. He opened the bottom drawer, dragged out the contents in one muddled heap and dropped it on the floor. Giles had time to see various brightly coloured shirts and jerseys and a worn pair of jeans before Martin pushed the whole lot under the bed with one sweep of his foot. Then he collapsed on the bed again as if the effort had exhausted him.

'Help yourself,' he said.

Giles was disturbed. 'Well, that's not really fair on you . . .' he began.

30

'No,' agreed Martin from the bed. 'Makes you weep, doesn't it? No one's fair to poor little Martin. Then you come in and pinch my drawer ...' He rolled over and hid his face in his pillow. He even made a queer sound like a sob.

Giles was almost sure he was joking, but not absolutely certain. He said, 'I could quite well keep my stuff in my case. I don't need the drawer really.'

Martin rolled on his back again. 'Do me a favour, kid,' he said. 'Just put your clobber in the drawer, will you? And don't be such a drip.' He searched around under the pillow until he found a squashed packet of cigarettes and started to smoke. Giles opened his case and quietly packed his clothes into the drawer.

The room was quiet for a while, but not very long. Martin started humming to himself, and a few minutes later got up and fetched the guitar down from the top of the wardrobe. He strummed some chords on it and sang, 'Crazy 'bout loving, Yea, yea. Crazy like crazy ...'

'Yea, yea, yea!' said Giles who was watching with interest and sitting on the edge of the bed.

Martin stopped with one hand held in the air. 'Do you realize you're sitting on my bed?'

Giles stood up. 'I'm sorry,' he said. 'I suppose I thought if I was going to use this room too ...'

'For sleeping in,' said Martin in a cold voice.

'Well, yes, but ...'

'You weren't thinking of sleeping just yet?'

'No, of course not.'

Martin trailed his fingers slowly across the strings

31

of the guitar. 'Some blokes will be coming up here pretty soon,' he said. 'To practise, like. You'd be in the way, see?'

Giles did not quite know what to say. He had that awkward feeling of knowing that he ought to get up and go, and yet did not know how to do it.

'Practise?' he said in a silly sort of voice. 'You mean music?'

'We've got a group,' Martin said in a bored sort of way. 'We bang about.'

'I'd like that,' Giles said. 'I could squeeze up in a corner somewhere.'

'We use all the corners,' said Martin. 'You don't get it, do you? I just said you'd be in the way. How many times do I have to tell you?'

'Oh, sorry,' said Giles. He was standing and all he had to do was walk to the door, but somehow he didn't seem able to. Then there was the sound of feet on the stairs, boys' voices, and laughing. The door opened and three boys came in, big boys about Martin's age, one of them carrying a guitar in a case. They shouted out meaningless words at Martin.

'How did you get in?' Martin asked.

'Twitch showed us right up,' said the one with the guitar.

Somehow Giles guessed that Twitch was their nickname for Linda and this amused him.

'Why do you call her Twitch?' he asked.

Martin and two of the boys acted as if he hadn't spoken; they went on laughing and joking together. The fourth boy, who had gone straight to the drums

32

and was arranging them on their stands, glanced across at him. 'What did you say, kid?'

'Why do you call her Twitch?'

'Because she twitches. Like when she laughs. Haven't you noticed?'

'I don't know her very well,' said Giles.

'Well, you watch her.'

Martin called across the room, 'Haven't you gone yet?'

Giles looked at the boy arranging the drums, hoping perhaps that he would speak up for him, but the boy was tapping lightly with one of the sticks on the side of the drum making a dry wooden sound and staring out of the window with an empty expression on his face. Giles slipped quietly out of the door and closed it behind him.

He stood for a few minutes on the stairs and suddenly the practice started. Three guitars, the drums, and four voices all at the same time. On the narrow stairway the sound was earsplitting, so Giles put his fingers in his ears and ran downstairs and into the sitting-room as fast as he could go.

Mr Maxwell had put the sewing-machine away and was laying the table for tea. Mrs Maxwell was out in the kitchen. Linda was still in the armchair reading the magazine, and Mr Judd had gone.

Only Linda seemed to notice him. She looked up from her magazine and said, 'Well, how did you get on with Martin?'

'Oh,' said Giles, not sure what to say, 'all right, I suppose.'

'I bet he threw you out though,' she said jeeringly.

Giles shrugged his shoulders comically.

Linda laughed, and Giles noticed that she brought one knee up in a queer jerky movement as she did so. That was what the drummer must have meant. He was on the point of saying something about it when it struck him she might not know the nickname they had for her, so stopped in time. Instead he said, 'The boy who played the drums seemed rather nice.'

Linda made a grimace. 'He's got ginger hair and freckles!' she said. 'I hate people with freckles.'

'Why?'

'I don't know. I just like boys to look sort of dark and savage,' she said. Then she went back to her magazine, full of boys with dark and savage looks probably.

'What's his name?' asked Giles.

'Who?'

'The drummer?'

'Oh him! Gribby.'

Mrs Maxwell's voice came from the kitchen. 'Linda! Help your father to lay the table, then.'

'He's almost finished,' Linda shouted back, not moving.

Mr Maxwell went on laying the table without saying anything.

4 Trouble over breakfast

Giles woke early the next morning; before it was properly light. He had been sleeping on the inside of the big bed, touching the wall some of the time because Martin was a restless sleeper and sprawled his arms and legs all over the bed. He gently lifted the edge of the curtain to see what it was like outside. It was a murky grey. The roof of the next door house was a black line against the dark grey sky. There were no stars. He let the curtain fall back into place. It was no use trying to get off to sleep again, so he wriggled into as comfortable a position as he could without waking Martin and stared at the dark ceiling.

How queer it was. Four completely strange people in a strange house; people he had never met before yesterday. And yet he was expected to behave like one of the family straight away. He did not even know what happened in the mornings. What time did they all get up? What sort of breakfasts did they usually have? Where was the school, and what would it be like?

When he remembered that he would have to start

35

at a new school that morning, Giles had an unpleasant, cold feeling that ran right down into his legs and feet. New schools were always awful. And the only boys who wanted to be friends were the ones who had no friends anyway, and either cadged things off you or got you into trouble in the first few days. Giles decided not to think of that for a while.

He must have wriggled without knowing it, for Martin grunted and kicked a leg out in his sleep, so that Giles had even less of the bed to lie in.

Martin! That was going to be his worst trouble. Martin obviously didn't like giving up any part of his room. He had been quite horrible the night before. Giles decided not to think of that either. In fact, when he came to it, there weren't many things he did want to think about just then. He didn't really want to lie there waiting till morning at all. He always liked to get straight out of bed when he woke up, but here everything was strange and different. Perhaps after a week or so he would feel more at home, but at the moment he found that hard to believe.

Just then he heard faint sounds from downstairs. Very faint they were, but saucepan noises and now and then the tap of crockery. Very carefully and slowly he sat up and pulled himself up on to the pillow, holding the covers down so that the cold air did not rush in and wake Martin up. Then he crept on hands and knees down the bed, feeling first with his fingers to make sure that he didn't put his weight on one of Martin's sprawled-out legs.

It took him quite a long time to reach the foot of the

bed. He climbed over it, edged across the room and slipped out of the door without any sign of life from Martin. Sure enough, there was a light downstairs; a thin slit of it shone through the gap in the sitting-room doorway. And the noises from the kitchen sounded louder from the stairs.

Giles wasn't at all sure what anyone would say to him, creeping down like this. After all, it might be the sort of house where children were expected to stay in bed until some special time. He just didn't know. Still, he wasn't going back now, so he went quietly down the stairs, through the sitting-room and into the kitchen.

He had half-thought to find Mrs Maxwell getting the breakfast, but he was not really surprised to see that it was Mr Maxwell, fully dressed with his shirt-sleeves rolled up, standing at the sink washing up. Giles stood for a few seconds, wondering what to say. Then he saw the wiping-up cloths hanging over the hot-water pipe near the boiler stove, so he took one and went over to the draining board.

Mr Maxwell glanced sideways and saw him. Giles picked up three plates together and started to wipe them dry.

'Up early then?' Mr Maxwell said, looking back at the washing-up water again and going on with the job.

Giles smiled and made a grunting sort of noise. He glanced round the kitchen, wondering where to put the dry plates.

'Bottom shelf in the cupboard,' said Mr Maxwell

as if reading his thought. 'And cups on the hooks. Do you like drying up, then?'

'Not much,' said Giles honestly.

'I hate washing up,' said Mr Maxwell. 'So that makes a pair of us, doesn't it?'

The tiled floor was cold to his feet, but otherwise the kitchen seemed a warm and friendly place. For once Giles found he quite enjoyed wiping up. Neither of them spoke again until it was all done. Then Mr Maxwell filled a kettle and put it on the gas.

'Feel like a cup of tea?' said Mr Maxwell.

'Yes, please.'

'You've earned it, too.'

While the kettle was boiling Mr Maxwell wiped all the bright coloured plastic surfaces in the kitchen clean and shiny and Giles finished putting the rest of the washed crockery away. Then they sat down on the kitchen stools on either side of the small red table and drank their tea. Giles could not remember when tea had ever tasted so good before.

'Best time of the day,' said Mr Maxwell. He looked at Giles for a moment. 'You warm enough?' he asked.

Giles nodded. He did not want to speak. For the last five or ten minutes he'd felt so much at home that he didn't want to spoil it. And speaking often did spoil things. People didn't always understand what you meant when you tried to put things into words. Better not to. Right now he would have liked to say something to Mr Maxwell about how much he liked him, but he knew that he would say it wrong and then nothing would be the same.

38

When they had finished their tea they washed and dried their cups and Mr Maxwell looked at the clock. 'You've just got time to run upstairs and change,' he said, 'while I cook some breakfast. That is if you'd like some now. The others don't start to wake up for another half hour or so when I usually take them up a morning cup of tea in bed.'

'Why do you have your breakfast so early then?' asked Giles.

'I have to be at work by eight. I can't hang about for the others. But you can wait if you want.'

'I'd rather have it with you,' Giles said, and ran off to get dressed. When he came down again Mr Maxwell had two rashers of bacon and two eggs sizzling in the pan and was putting three cups on a tray ready to take upstairs. 'Just in time,' he said and scooped the food off on to two plates.

But before they could sit down to it there was a noise on the stairs and Mrs Maxwell came in wearing a pretty pink dressing-gown, yawning and tousling her hair with her fingers.

'I wondered who you could be talking to this time of the morning,' she said to her husband. 'Never struck me it might be him.'

'Giles helped me with the washing up,' said Mr Maxwell. 'Proper little worker he is.'

'What washing up?' said Mrs Maxwell. 'I did all the washing up before I went to bed last night.'

'Just a few odds and ends,' said Mr Maxwell.

Giles could not understand what made him say this. There had been heaps and heaps. All the supper things for a start.

Mrs Maxwell sat down at the table and looked at the breakfast that was to have been Giles'. 'How nice,' she said. 'I must come down early more often. I don't usually have my breakfast cooked for me.'

She picked up the knife and fork and started to eat with obvious enjoyment. 'You'd better have yours if you're not going to be late for work,' she said to her husband.

There was a moment of dreadful silence. Mr Maxwell did not seem to know what to say. Before any

40

words came Giles blurted out, 'Well, I'm going to
to get my morning breath of fresh air. Shan't be long!'

'You must be mad,' said Mrs Maxwell, folding up
the bacon and smothering it with egg yolk.

'Well, look . . .' began Mr Maxwell.

'Cheerio,' said Giles and dashed off before another
word could be said.

Outside the air was cold and raw and Giles realized
that he ought to have put a coat on. It was too late
now, though. He'd just have to trot to keep warm.
So he broke into a gentle trot, up the street towards
the main road then along to the left, waiting for the
next street, so that he could run round a sort of square
and get back to the house again. He did not need to
be out very long. Once Mr Maxwell had actually
started to eat his breakfast everything would be all
right. Giles had a marvellous warm feeling inside him.
He felt very pleased with the quick way he had acted,
so that no one should feel awkward about there being
two breakfasts for three people. He wondered what
Mr Maxwell would be thinking to himself. Probably
thinking nice friendly things about him.

He came to the left-hand turn and ran down it.
His hands were going a bit blue, but otherwise he was
feeling quite warm. Anyway he would be back inside
in a little while. How nice it had been in the kitchen
with just him and Mr Maxwell, friendly and cosy
over the washing up and a cup of tea. Giles thought
to himself that it would be rather nice to get up early
like that every morning.

All the streets and all the houses were the same in

this place, but here was another turn to the left and that should take him back somewhere near the Maxwells' house. He turned down it. A few minutes' running brought him into another street, and sure enough he was only about fifty yards from the house. Just as well because he was puffed and couldn't have run much farther.

He went round the house because the front door was shut, and shot through the kitchen door, shut it behind him and leaned against it, puffing noisily and trying to get his breath. Things were swimming a little before his eyes and he made out vaguely that Mr and Mrs Maxwell were both standing up. Mr Maxwell had his coat and hat on – probably just off to work. Giles shut his eyes for a moment, feeling the warmth of the kitchen and seeing a cloud of odd tiny green specks floating like shooting stars across the insides of his closed eyelids.

'No need to make such a fuss about it!' said Mrs Maxwell's voice, loudly and angrily. 'Anyone could make a mistake! You only had to say!'

'You ought to have seen for yourself,' shouted Mr Maxwell. 'Anyone with half an ounce of sense . . .'

'Are you trying to say I'm stupid?' cried Mrs Maxwell furiously.

Giles suddenly realized with a dreadful shock that he had plunged back into the middle of a quarrel. He opened his eyes and saw that both of them were staring at each other with angry expressions on their faces.

'I'm off!' said Mr Maxwell and pushing past Giles

as if he had not seen him went out and slammed the door behind him.

Giles looked at the table and saw to his amazement that while Mrs Maxwell seemed to have eaten one of the breakfasts, the other one was untouched – going cold and greasy on the plate. Mr Maxwell couldn't have had anything to eat at all.

'Oh, you're back then!' exclaimed Mrs Maxwell in a very cross voice. 'You're a fine one, you are. Causing trouble on your very first morning. Why couldn't you stay in bed like other people?'

Giles felt quite dizzy with this. He was not at all sure what he had done wrong. 'I didn't mean . . .' he stuttered.

'Why didn't you say that was your breakfast?' she asked. 'You only had to say it. I didn't mean to take your breakfast. Oh no. Instead of just saying it, like any normal person would, you go dashing out of the door and let me go on eating it without knowing.'

'I thought . . .' said Giles.

'Think how silly I felt,' she went on, taking no notice of his efforts to answer. 'When I'd eaten the last mouthful Doug tells me. I ask you! Make me feel a proper monster. Well that's a good start, I must say.'

Giles realized that it was no use trying to say anything. He just stared at her miserably and waited for it all to finish.

'If you'd only said something!' Mrs Maxwell repeated. 'But no, you go running off and . . .'

Giles heard it all in a daze. He had stopped listening to the actual words long ago. He was thinking that

43

Mr Maxwell must have gone off to work without any breakfast. It made him feel dreadful. Mrs Maxwell went on being cross with him for what seemed hours, but at last she stopped talking and went back upstairs to dress. The last thing she said as she went was:

'Since there's been so much fuss about it, you'd better eat that breakfast, that's all I can say. No reason to waste good food.'

Giles sat down at the table and looked at the plate, but the thought of trying to eat the half-cold egg and bacon made him feel quite sick. After a few minutes he scraped it off the plate into the top of the boiler fire. Then he washed the plate up, dried it, and put it away. Rather like a criminal getting rid of the evidence, he thought to himself.

He was just wondering what to do and whether he would get into trouble if he looked around for the shoe-cleaning things, when the back door opened again and it was Mr Maxwell.

'Forgot my thermos,' he said.

He came across the kitchen and took the thermos flask from the back of the draining board. Giles wanted very much to say something but could not think of the words. He simply watched Mr Maxwell turn and walk towards the back door again. At the door, however, Mr Maxwell stopped and looked at him.

'We made a proper mess of that breakfast between us, didn't we?' he said. His voice sounded quite cheerful and not at all cross.

'But you didn't get any,' Giles exclaimed.

'I'll get something at the canteen,' said Mr Maxwell.

'Don't you worry about me. Oh, and look! Good luck at school today! I know what it's like starting some-where fresh.'

With that he was gone, but Giles felt quite different. He felt as if he had been wandering around lost in a huge wood for hours and hours, and then had sud-denly come to a part that he knew quite well and that was in fact only a little way from home.

5 *A sort of cousin*

Haleshangar Secondary School was not in the village but rather more than half a mile out of it. It was a very modern school, with a great deal of glass, shaped like a number of boxes, one standing up on end and the others lying on their sides. It had a large playing field to one side, a small farm behind the gardens, and greenhouses at the other side.

The school stood all by itself in the middle of all its land and seemed immense to Giles as he and Linda walked together up the main road towards it. Giles felt his tummy beginning to flutter at the mere sight of it.

'It's so huge!' he complained miserably. 'I hate big schools. I shan't know anyone, and I'll keep getting lost for weeks and weeks.'

Linda wasn't much comfort. 'When I first went there,' she said, 'our whole class got lost three or four times a day the first week. Once we were lost for so long they had to send out a search party, and they found us all standing in the medical room waiting for a science lesson. We did feel silly.'

'At least there were a lot of you all together,' Giles said. 'When I get lost I'll be all by myself.'

They were at the gate by this time. Giles took a deep breath as if he was going to dive into cold water. 'Well, here goes,' he muttered and followed Linda in.

Half a dozen girls standing just inside the gate surrounded them immediately, all talking to Linda at once. They all looked at Giles as if he was some sort of rare animal brought back from the jungle, but none of them actually spoke to him. They spoke about him, though, much to Giles' embarrassment.

'Who's he, then?' he heard one of them say.

'Linda, who's that boy?' said another.

'He's quite nice when he frowns,' said a third.

Giles gave this one a really ferocious scowl; she squealed and grabbed Linda's arm. She had very long, dark hair, done up in a sort of knot on the top of her head, and Giles heard the other girls calling her Sandra. He walked more slowly so that the girls went on ahead. Linda seemed to have forgotten about him for the moment. There were groups of boys and girls standing about the playground. Giles saw them only in a sort of a blur. He knew all the faces would be strange to him, so it was no use staring to see if any of them knew him. He supposed vaguely he ought to go to the headmaster's room first and wondered where it could be. No good looking himself, and he didn't dare go up to anyone to ask the way.

The girls were farther away now and he stood still, rather like a tiny island in the middle of a huge sea. He felt so lonely that it hurt.

47

Standing there and looking at nothing, he did not notice the girl called Sandra coming towards him. She made him jump when she spoke.

'I say! Linda says you'd better go and see the headmaster. Shall I show you where his office is?'

'Oh,' said Giles. He was surprised to see that she was quite embarrassed too. 'Oh, yes. All right, then. And ... thanks.'

'Come on then,' she said.

She led the way through a side door into the school and then along various corridors and up stairs and round corners. Neither of them said anything and Giles kept half a step behind Sandra all the way. He tried hard to remember the way so that he could get back to the playground if necessary without getting lost. I ought to have brought a ball of thread with me, he thought, remembering the old Greek story of Theseus and the Minotaur.

At last they came to a door with three lights over the top, green, amber, and red. The amber one was lit up.

'See those lights,' Sandra said. 'The green one means you can knock and walk in. The amber one means you're to wait, and the red one means either he's too busy to see anyone or he's gone out. Crafty, isn't it?'

Giles nodded and swallowed hard. His mouth seemed to have gone very dry suddenly.

'I'll wait with you a moment,' Sandra said. Then a moment later, 'Linda says you're staying at their place for a time.'

48

'Yes,' said Giles. The odd way his throat felt wouldn't let him say any more.

'She said you were some sort of relative. Sort of cousin, I suppose.'

'Oh,' said Giles, taken by surprise. 'She said that, did she?' He felt warm and friendly towards Linda for saying that; he couldn't quite understand why. Anyway it meant she wasn't ashamed of him.

'Aren't you, then?' asked Sandra.

'A sort of cousin? Well, yes. Linda said so, didn't she?'

Sandra had a puzzled little frown for a moment, but it went almost immediately. 'Have you heard the Minors?' she said.

'The Minors?'

'Martin's group. They play guitars and that. I think they're smashing. Better than half the groups you see on the telly.'

'I heard them practising last night,' Giles said.

'Weren't they smashing?'

Giles was trying to decide what to say when the lights over the headmaster's door changed to green.

'That's it, then,' Sandra said. 'Just knock once and walk in. Good luck!'

Giles pulled his jacket down hard, swallowed twice, rapped on the door – much too loud, he thought – and walked in.

'Well, well, well,' said the headmaster. 'Giles Willis, isn't it? You've grown a bit since I last saw you. So now you're going to be here with us, eh?'

'Mr Norton!' exclaimed Giles. 'I didn't know . . .'

He found it hard to believe that here was someone he actually knew. As a matter of fact Giles had met Mr Norton under rather violent circumstances; he had been knocked down by Mr Norton's car in the road just outside the Home. Giles had been in hospital as a result, for six weeks with a broken leg. And during the time he had been there Mr Norton had called to see him at least four times a week and had brought him books, sweets, and fruit. What was more he had wanted to know all about Giles himself, about his life, what it was like living in a Home, what had happened to his parents, what he liked doing in his spare time, and so on. In fact Giles had talked more to Mr Norton in those few weeks than he ever had to anybody else in the world. Giles did not have any friends, but Mr Norton was about the nearest thing to a friend.

Now, in the headmaster's room, they sat and talked for about ten minutes until a loud bell rang somewhere in the school and Mr Norton hurriedly glanced up at the clock on the wall and said, 'That's for assembly, and I haven't done any of the things I ought to have done. Look, come down to the hall now, and after assembly you can come back here and we'll fix up which class you'll be in, and any other official business that's necessary. All right?'

Giles grinned. 'If I can find my way,' he said.

'We'll look after that,' said Mr Norton, opening the door and striding out into the corridor. 'Do you want to see me, Sandra?' he asked, finding the girl standing near his door.

'Oh, well . . . no, sir. Not exactly,' said Sandra, looking embarrassed.

'What exactly do you want, then?'

Sandra went quite scarlet. 'Him!' she said, nodding at Giles. 'I brought him up here, sir, and I thought I'd better wait for him in case he got lost again when he came out.'

'That was kind of you,' Mr Norton said. 'Now you can take him down to the hall for assembly, and bring him back again here afterwards. And thank you.'

Giles followed Sandra down the corridor. As soon as they turned the first corner she collapsed against the wall and fanned her face with her hand. 'He would come out and catch me,' she exclaimed. 'I never felt so silly in my life.'

Giles was not sure what to say to make her feel more comfortable. In the end he said, 'Thank you for waiting for me, anyway.'

'Oh, I've got a very kind heart,' she said.

'I'm sure you have,' said Giles, not sure whether to take this seriously or not.

Sandra clenched her fist and held it very close under his nose. 'You laugh at me,' she said threateningly, 'and you'll get this right on the end of your hooter!'

Giles backed a little in alarm. 'I didn't mean . . .'

'Maybe not,' she said. 'But don't try it, see? Now come on or we'll be late.' And with that she went off at high speed down stairs and round corners and down corridors, so that Giles had almost to run to keep her in sight. Some girl! he thought to himself, somewhat shaken by the whole business.

51

Assembly passed with Giles still in a daze. So many hundreds of faces, so much noise, prayers, hymns, readings, music, they all passed over his head and he only really shook himself out of it again when he found himself back in Mr Norton's study.

'I think I'll put you in A2 for a start,' the Head was saying. 'You're living with the Maxwells, aren't you? Well, Linda is in that class. She can keep an eye on you. She's quite a nice girl – better than that lazy brother of hers.'

Giles said nothing.

'I suppose he hasn't got a job yet?' Mr Norton said.

'Martin? No, not yet. He runs a dance band though.'

'Does he? What is it like?'

Giles was on the point of saying something nasty when he checked himself. 'They make a lot of noise,' he said.

'They wouldn't be much of a band if they didn't,' said Mr Norton with a laugh. 'And what about the Maxwells? Do you like them?'

'I'm more concerned about whether they like me,' said Giles.

'Well you shouldn't be. If you like them you can be sure they'll like you.'

'You mean I ought to make myself like them?'

'No, but you could start by looking for the good things about them first.'

Giles thought about this on and off during the day. He wasn't at all sure it made sense. So many things that adults said you ought to do turned out to be impossible. It was all very well to say he should like the Maxwells. What about them? He thought of them one at a time. Linda was all right. Nothing special, but she had told Sandra he was a relation and that was rather nice of her. But on the other hand she was bossy and . . . He stopped himself at that point. You couldn't get to like someone if you thought of the bad points. That was the first thing to remember. Think of the nice things and go on from there.

So Linda was all right. And Mr Maxwell was all right; Giles already liked him quite a lot, especially after that little session in the kitchen. But what about the other two? Mrs Maxwell had told him off and Martin couldn't stand the sight of him. How would Mr Norton get round those two? It was easy enough to talk!

After school Giles waited for Linda. After about ten minutes she came out with Sandra and two other girls and walked past him without even noticing that he was there.

6 Practice for the group

That evening after tea Giles said to Linda, 'I've got some homework to do.'

'Well, so have I, haven't I?'

'I know. I didn't mean quite that. I was going to say, where's the best place to do it?'

Linda shrugged. 'Anywhere you can find a place. Sometimes I do mine in the sitting-room. But if I can't concentrate because of the telly, I either go into the kitchen or up into my room.'

Giles knew he would never be able to work with the television on, and as Mr Maxwell was in the kitchen tinkering with some electrical stuff he had brought home from work, he took his books up into the bedroom. Martin had gone off after tea, so for a time at least he had the bedroom to himself.

He worked hard for almost an hour, taking great pains with the exercises because he wanted to make a good impression at his new school. He had finished the English and was about half-way through mathematics when the crashing of boots on the stairs and the sound of boys laughing told him Martin was on his way up with his group. It was no good trying to work with them in the room – even supposing they would let him stay there – so he began to pack his books up.

'You're here, are you, then?' said Martin, coming into the room first.

'I'm just going. I had some homework to do.'

'Homework!' Martin made a contemptuous noise. 'I never used to do any. I don't approve of homework. What I say is, if you can't get it done between nine and four, there must be something wrong with the school. It's up to them to put it right, not make the kids do overtime because they're so badly organized.'

'I don't mind it,' said Giles.

'Don't listen to him, kid,' said the ginger-haired drummer. 'Old Martin never used to do any work in school time either. He's dead lazy.'

As he said this he stopped to look over Giles' shoulder at the open maths book.

'Look who's talking!' jeered Martin, squatting back on his bed and striking a few chords on his guitar. 'I don't remember you taking any prizes at the end of the year!'

The drummer took no notice of this; he was looking at Giles' work. 'Used to be my favourite subject,' he said to Giles. 'I was pretty good at maths. You're not bad yourself, are you?'

'Are we going to start, or aren't we?' said Martin.

The drummer did not move. 'You made a mistake in that second one, though,' he said to Giles. 'You didn't allow for the thickness of the metal, did you...?'

'Stone the crows!' Martin burst out in an angry

55

voice. 'We didn't come up here to natter about school homework, did we? Look, get those books out of here, will you? Get running, or I'll chuck the lot out of the window . . .'

'Take it easy, you great ape!' said the drummer in a good-humoured voice. 'Do you want to eat the kid or something?'

'I just want him out!' growled Martin.

'Come on, Gribby,' said one of the other boys. 'Let's get started!'

Giles hurriedly thrust his books into his satchel, thinking at the same time that it needed a genius to find anything likeable in Martin. Still, it was no use hanging around making trouble. Before he reached the door, however, the drummer, Gribby, said to him quietly:

'Hang on, kid. What's your name? Giles, isn't it? Well look! Why don't you stay up here a while and listen to us. See what you think, eh?'

Giles looked across to see how Martin was taking this, but Gribby said, 'Don't look at him; this is a democracy. I just asked you a question.'

'Well . . .' began Giles doubtfully.

'You want his expert opinion, I suppose?' jeered Martin.

'Do us good to play to an audience,' said Gribby. 'Anyway, why shouldn't he stay? It's partly his room, isn't it?'

There was a silence after he'd said this. Martin seemed on the point of some angry outburst, then he shrugged his shoulders and started fiddling with the tuning of his guitar. 'Please yourself – I don't care,' he muttered.

'Right. Tuck yourself away in a corner,' said Gribby. 'And hold on to something – we make a fair noise when we get going.'

Giles did not take the last part seriously, but he did get well out of everybody's way, sitting in fact on the far side of the bed with his back against the wall and both legs doubled under him. He watched with great interest as the guitars were tuned and wires plugged into them that led back to the complicated-looking apparatus by the wall. Gribby was setting up his drum-kit, fussing a little as he made sure that each part, drum or cymbal or temple block or whatever it was, stood exactly the right distance from him, around in a half circle. He had a little drum break all to himself to test them out while the others were twanging notes and checking that the right amount of noise came from the two loud-speakers.

'Right, then,' said Martin. 'Gently for a start, eh boys? Just a whisper on the drums, man. And keep it light after the intro. One, two . . .'

Three slow notes came from the lowest string of Martin's bass guitar, dropping sadly down, so low and so sad, like weeping, the last note sounding very loud through the speakers and held there. Giles could feel it more than he could hear it. Then a pause and the soft whisper of the brushes across the drum and the tune played very quietly as if the sound were being carried away through the trees by the wind. Martin sang, quietly, as if he really was sad:

57

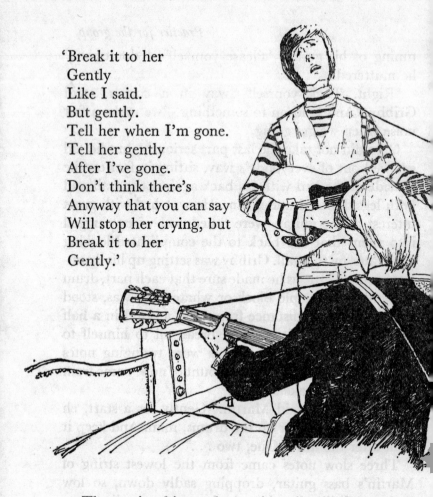

'Break it to her
Gently
Like I said.
But gently.
Tell her when I'm gone.
Tell her gently
After I've gone.
Don't think there's
Anyway that you can say
Will stop her crying, but
Break it to her
Gently.'

The music whispered away into silence. Giles wasn't sure whether he ought to clap or not, and while he was still wondering, the group crashed into their next number. Crashed it was. The drums went mad, the guitars throbbed like breakers pounding on the beach, the very roof seemed to be falling in on top of them. Even the words, which all the boys howled

58

together, did not make any sort of sense, but were hurled into the air like a handful of gravel at a glass window. Giles found himself bouncing on the back of the bed in time with the beat. He seemed to be caught up in some sort of rhythmical thunderstorm, tossed first this way by the drums, then that way by the wild chords and the harsh voices.

Second-hand Family

And suddenly it had finished and there was a dead silence. The group seemed to droop over their instruments as if they were exhausted.

Before he had realized it Giles had cried out, 'That was smashing. It was fabulous. It really was!' He still felt the excitement of it and knelt up on the bed, staring first at one boy then another.

'Well, thanks,' said Martin, and it was hard to tell whether he meant it or was being his usual sarcastic self.

'Fame comes at last!' said Gribby, with a grin.

The words were hardly out of his mouth before there was rhythmical thump-thump-thump on the wall just behind the speakers. Thump-thump-thump as if someone was getting to work with a broom or a mop on the other side of the wall.

'Applause from the neighbours!' said Martin and struck a couple of very low, loud notes on his guitar.

From the other side of the wall came a faint, but obviously angry voice:

'If you lot don't turn it in I'll phone for the police!'

'They want an encore!' said Martin. 'What shall we give them? How about this . . .?'

He struck up the first notes of 'Crazy 'bout loving' and the others joined in good and loud. It was impossible to tell if the neighbours kept up their objection because the music in the little room was too loud to let in any other sound. Giles thought he heard a faint wail from somewhere in the distance, but it was drowned out immediately by the next 'yea, yea, yea'. He jumped up and down on the bed, joining in the

60

song when he remembered the words. It was like being in a battle. And the boys grinned at each other and then at Giles almost as if he was one of them.

The music ended and they all listened. There was no more objection from the neighbours next door.

'Seems to have fixed them,' said Martin. 'Well, now what? Shall we run through that new number?'

They started again on a tune Giles had never heard before. And this time, instead of playing it straight through, they played a little bit, then talked about it and played the same bit again two or three times in different ways, making suggestions to each other. Giles found this a little boring and was just wishing they would play something properly when the bedroom door burst open and Mrs Maxwell came into the room looking absolutely furious.

'This is a fine thing!' she exclaimed.

All the boys stopped playing and looked at her.

'What did you say, Mum?' said Martin.

'I suppose you didn't hear the thumping on the wall!' she said angrily. 'Didn't strike you that there might be somebody who didn't like the row you were making!'

'You know what the neighbours round here are like,' said Martin. 'Grumble about anything, some of them.'

'I'm the one that has to meet them next day,' said Mrs Maxwell. 'Well, Mr Whiting's at the front door this very moment.'

'Him!' said Martin contemptuously.

'Yes, him. And he says he's going straight to the police if you play another note.'

'He's a good one to complain,' cried Martin. 'When he rows with his wife the whole street can hear it . . .'

Mrs Maxwell interrupted furiously. 'I'm not arguing about it, Martin. And I'm not having the police at this house on your account. You don't even pay me your keep, and yet you think the house belongs to you and we just have to put up with the way you go on. Well, you can all clear out! See? This very moment! Not another sound out of you.'

She stood away from the door and held it wide open as if she thought they would all walk straight out.

'I'm sorry, Mrs Maxwell . . .' Gribby said. 'I guess we just weren't thinking . . .'

'I'm waiting!' said Mrs Maxwell grimly.

'We could practise round my place,' said one of the boys.

'How can we?' said Martin. 'We've got all the gear here, haven't we?'

'We'll just have to give it a miss tonight,' Gribby said. 'And work something out tomorrow. Come on, you blokes!'

He stood up and made for the door. 'Good night, Mrs Maxwell!' he added as he passed her. She said nothing but continued to stare angrily at the others who sheepishly unplugged their guitars and then edged past her in the narrow doorway, rather as if they thought she might bite them. Martin busied himself with coiling up cable, switching off the apparatus and putting his guitar away. He didn't look up at his mother again and after a few minutes she went, shutting the door very firmly behind her.

For a few minutes there was absolute silence in the bedroom. Giles was sitting as if turned to stone. He'd thought Mrs Maxwell had been angry with him that morning, but that had been nothing at all compared with the stormy fury that had just swept the room. He found he was still holding his breath and let it out now in a sort of sigh. And there was Martin calmly tidying up as if nothing had happened.

Martin heard Giles sigh and looked up with a grin. 'You can breathe again now,' he said.

'I was scared stiff,' Giles admitted.

'Oh, you don't want to take too much notice of Mum,' Martin said. 'She does her top now and then, but it's all over in a few minutes. She's as right as rain after.'

'But where are you going to practise if you can't do it here?' said Giles.

'Who says we can't do it here? The boys'll be round tomorrow, you'll see, just as if nothing had happened. They know Mum. Why, if they didn't turn up she'd be the first one to start asking where they'd got to. You just don't know Mum yet.'

Giles felt he certainly didn't know Mrs Maxwell very well yet.

'One good thing,' Martin said. 'You can finish your homework in peace now.'

'Homework? Oh, yes,' said Giles and very slowly got his case open and his books out again. He felt he was going to find it hard to settle to maths again after all that excitement.

7 *An evening's bingo*

Some days later, at tea-time, Linda said to Giles, 'Go on, Giles, why don't you tell him?'

Giles shot a quick look at Martin who was sitting, both elbows on the table, scooping food into his mouth with quick, hungry movements.

'Not just now,' he mumbled.

'Do you have to eat like that?' said Mrs Maxwell sharply. 'If you could just see yourself! Look how nicely Giles is sitting. He quite shows you up.'

Martin sneered and leaned even farther over his plate. 'Better send me to a Home to teach me good manners then,' he said.

Not knowing where to look in his embarrassment, Giles stared at the rim of his cup.

'Why not just now?' said Linda loudly. 'I think you ought to tell him. He'll be pleased.'

Giles tried to give her a gentle kick under the table, but she jumped in the air and shrieked as if she had a broken ankle at least. 'What was that for?' she cried.

'I think Giles was trying to persuade you to shut up!' said Mr Maxwell, with a slight smile. He thought that Giles had broken something and Linda was pushing him to own up about it. He was quite wrong in fact; it was to Martin that Giles had something to confess.

A couple of days before Martin had been quite friendly with Giles, but now he seemed quite the opposite. Especially after what Mrs Maxwell had just said. Giles did not want to provoke him any further. However, Linda wouldn't let the matter rest.

'If you're not going to say anything, then I shall,' she announced.

'Better get it off your chest, old chap,' Mr Maxwell said.

'I don't understand what you're all talking about,' said Mrs Maxwell. 'Is it some secret? Do tell him – don't tell him! Who's him, anyway?'

'Martin,' said Linda. 'Giles did something today and he's got to tell Martin about it.'

'It's nothing to do with you,' said Giles, wishing she'd stop nagging him.

'Oh, no! Not much! You've only made it so that everybody in the class will be laughing at me, that's all.'

'I don't see that at all,' persisted Giles, not very wisely as it turned out.

'Oh, don't you? Well, I'll soon show you.' Linda was certainly being extremely awkward. 'You only told old Mars Bar that Martin would bring his group down to the school and play for us. And you hadn't even asked Martin first, and what's more, if I hadn't said anything about it, Martin wouldn't even have known.

65

And anyway he won't bring the group down. Any fool could have told you Martin won't take his group down to the school, not even if you paid him. So obviously they're all going to laugh at me.'

'Who in heaven's name is old Mars Bar?' asked Mrs Maxwell.

Martin however brushed her aside. He stood up and glared down at Giles. 'You said I'd do *what*?' he demanded in a voice like coal sacks being emptied.

Giles was so nervous he could hardly speak properly. How he hated Linda at that moment. He had wanted to pick just the right time to talk to Martin, but Linda had done it all wrong and back to front and made a proper mess of it.

'Come on!' demanded Martin. 'Spill it out. You said I'd do what?'

'It wasn't quite the way Linda said,' stammered Giles.

'What way was it, then?'

'Well, Mars Bar was saying . . .'

'Won't someone tell me who Mars Bar is?' wailed Mrs Maxwell.

'Oh, Mum, do be quiet,' Linda said.

'It's Mr Marshall, the music-teacher,' said Giles. 'Well, he was saying there weren't any good tunes nowadays and about long-haired roughs banging on guitars and shouting at the tops of their voices and . . . oh you know the sort of thing people say . . .'

'I'm waiting to hear what *you* said,' Martin insisted.

'I said I didn't think he could ever have listened properly.'

66

'Ooh, you didn't!' exclaimed Mrs Maxwell. 'I shouldn't have thought you'd have had the nerve.'

Mr Maxwell put down his knife and fork, leaned back in his chair and laughed until he went red in the face and nearly choked himself. 'I'd like to have seen Marshall's face,' he spluttered.

Martin was the only one who was not amused. He leaned forward on the table and when his father had subsided he said, 'Yes, and then what?'

'Oh,' said Giles, 'then we got into a sort of argument and I said your group played music that was twice as good as any of the songs he tried to make us sing . . . and then I sort of offered . . . well, I sort of said . . .'

'What?' repeated Martin firmly.

Giles gulped. 'I said I'd ask you to bring the Minors down to the school so that he could see what I meant, and he said he thought that was a very good idea . . .' His voice trailed away as he said this and he looked miserably at Martin's face. It had seemed such a good idea at the time, but now . . .

'And you really thought,' said Martin, 'that the Minors would want to waste their time playing to a lot of screaming school kids? You really thought that?'

'It was a sort of argument,' mumbled Giles. 'I suppose I didn't really think . . .'

'That's it, then,' said Martin. 'You'd better tell Mr Marshall. And next time maybe you won't be so ready to fix things up without finding out first.'

'Now wait a minute,' said Mr Maxwell. 'Giles meant it as a sort of compliment, you know. After all, he was sticking up for you.'

67

'We don't need anybody to stick up for us, thanks.'

'All the same . . .'

'I'd be much obliged,' said Martin coldly, 'if you'd all mind your own business.' Then he marched out.

'There you are!' said Linda. 'I knew he'd be like that. It serves you right. Fancy promising . . .'

'I didn't promise!' cried Giles indignantly. 'And it might have been all right if you hadn't butted in. You just put him off, the way you told it.'

'Giles is right,' said Mr Maxwell. 'You're nothing but a mischief-maker, Linda.'

'Well, I like that . . .' spluttered Linda.

'I think it was a very good idea,' said Mrs Maxwell. 'I think Martin was most ungrateful.'

'Oh,' cried Linda, jumping to her feet. 'You're all against me. It's not fair!' Then she burst into tears and ran out of the room, slamming the door loudly behind her.

'Temper!' exclaimed Mrs Maxwell.

Giles felt rather like bursting into tears himself, but somehow managed to control himself. Everything had gone so beastly wrong. And it really had seemed a good idea at the time. All the kids in the class had thought so. They'd got quite excited. 'That'll be something like a music lesson,' some of them had said. And now they were all going to be disappointed.

Mr and Mrs Maxwell were both as decent as anything trying to cheer him up and make him feel that it hadn't been his fault. They couldn't change it though. Martin had been so furious at the idea, and he was the one that counted.

A little later when Mr Maxwell started to clear the table, Giles helped to carry the things out into the kitchen. Mrs Maxwell filled the basin at the sink and said, 'You don't need to do that. Why don't you get on with your homework?'

'I like doing it,' said Giles. 'Anyway I've only got about ten minutes' homework tonight.'

He helped Mr Maxwell dry and put away. It was very quiet and soothing in the kitchen, everyone busy and not talking. Now and then Giles caught the eye of one or other of his foster-parents and smiled. Each time Mrs Maxwell smiled back and Mr Maxwell winked.

'Well, that's the lot,' said Mrs Maxwell at last, drying her hands on her apron and then taking it off and hanging it behind the kitchen door. 'Could you get your homework done by half past seven?'

'Easily.'

'We were going down to the bingo at half past seven. Would you like to come with us?'

'I've never been to bingo.'

'Time you tried it then,' said Mr Maxwell.

'I'd like to,' said Giles.

'That's settled then,' said Mrs Maxwell. 'I'll just go and change my dress.'

Less than an hour later Mr and Mrs Maxwell, with Giles walking between them, were approaching the Welfare Hall. This was in the centre of the village; a new hall which the miners and their families used for all sorts of meetings and dances, parties, clubs, and of course bingo. It was warm and bright and noisy

69

inside. The whole of Haleshangar seemed to be there, sitting round little tables, laughing and talking.

Mr Maxwell went first, threading his way through the tables, looking for an empty one. Giles followed with Mrs Maxwell close behind. He felt very self-conscious; as if everyone there was watching him. He saw one or two familiar faces of children in his class at school, but his face seemed to have frozen into a solid sheet so that when they spoke to him he could not smile or answer, only nod his head at them in what he felt was a rather ridiculously dignified way. They'll think I'm awfully stuck-up, he thought.

To his relief he saw Mr Maxwell beckoning from a vacant table, and like a swimmer at the very end of his strength he reached it and sank into a chair. Mr and Mrs Maxwell, however, were in no hurry to sit down. They stood and looked round, smiling and waving and even shouting to various people they knew.

'It must be nice to know everybody,' Giles said as Mrs Maxwell at last sank down in the chair next to him.

'You'll know them all in a little while,' said Mrs Maxwell. 'They're just ordinary people, that's all. Nothing to be scared of.'

Giles was wondering to himself whether he was likely to stay in Haleshangar long enough to get to know many people. Before he could answer, however, a girl bobbed up from the next table but one and came across. It was Sandra, looking very grown-up, out of school uniform, and wearing nylon stockings and shoes with thin, pointed heels.

'Hullo, Mrs Maxwell,' she said, and smiled and nodded at Giles and Mr Maxwell. 'Isn't Linda coming tonight?'

'Linda's ... not feeling quite herself,' said Mrs Maxwell. 'Do you know Giles?'

'We're in the same class,' said Sandra. 'Here, did Giles tell you about his idea to get Martin and the Minors down to school for a music lesson?'

'Yes, we heard about it,' said Mr Maxwell.

'Wouldn't it be fabulous? Just imagine ...'

'It rather depends on Martin, doesn't it?' said Mr Maxwell, with a grin.

'I suppose it does. Giles will just about be torn to pieces, though, if he can't talk him into it.'

Giles gave a silly nervous giggle at this, but he was saved from having to think up some reply by a man at the far end of the hall asking everybody to sit down. Sandra plunged back to her table.

Although Giles had never played bingo before, he soon found that it was a very simple game. Someone called out numbers and when these were the same numbers that were printed on the card in front of you, you crossed them out. The first person with all the numbers crossed out won the game and was allowed to go up and choose one of the prizes that were spread out on a table at the end of the hall.

After the first three games Giles began to think it was rather dull and silly. He had less than half his numbers crossed out when someone jumped up from another table and waved his card to show he had finished. During the fourth game, however, every

71

number that was called was one on Giles' card, and as he crossed them out one after another he began to get excited.

'It's your lucky turn for sure this time!' whispered Mr Maxwell.

Finally Giles had just one number left, number seventy-three. It's the number of our house, he thought, it's bound to come up. He crossed his fingers under the table and waited excitedly for the next number. 'Bed and breakfast – twenty-six!' called the man, and then, 'All the twos – twenty-two.' Half a dozen more numbers were called, none of them the one Giles was waiting for, then a tall, bony woman with a face like a chopper jumped up and shouted, 'Bingo!'

'Of all the luck!' said Mrs Maxwell.

After that Giles began to lose interest again. He never got anywhere near winning again. After all, he thought to himself, it wasn't really a game. It was just luck. Just as he was thinking this Mrs Maxwell clutched his arm. 'Look!' she whispered.

Giles glanced at her card and saw that she had only two numbers left. 'Legs – eleven!' called the voice.

Mrs Maxwell had it. She handed Giles the pencil. 'You do it,' she said. 'My hand's too shaky.'

Giles crossed out the eleven and waited. It couldn't happen. Sixty-nine wanted. Someone else was bound to win. The woman with a face like a chopper, probably. She'd already won twice tonight.

'Sixty-nine!' said the voice.

'BINGO!' screamed Mrs Maxwell, snatching up the card and waving it wildly.

'Take it easy!' laughed Mr Maxwell, but his wife was already plunging through between the tables towards the end of the hall.

'She's had her eye on those linen table-cloths,' said Mr Maxwell, leaning back in his chair. 'What's the betting, eh?'

A few seconds later Mrs Maxwell was back again, flushed a little and panting. She put a pair of shining new roller skates down on the table.

'What do you want those for?' gasped Mr Maxwell.

'I thought Giles might like them,' she said.

Giles stared at the skates, hardly daring to touch them, hardly believing his ears. 'For me?'

'A little present,' said Mrs Maxwell.

'No one ever gave me a present like that before.'

'Then it's about time someone did,' she said.

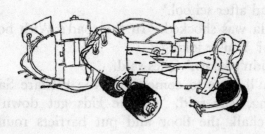

8 A date for the Minors

At breakfast the following morning Linda said, 'Well, let's see them.'

Giles produced the skates proudly but yet hesitantly. He thought Linda might be jealous that her mother had given her prize to Giles instead of to one of her own children.

Linda examined the skates with great care. 'They're real whizzy,' she said at last. 'Better than mine.' She said this without rancour. 'Can you skate?'

'Not yet,' said Giles. 'I thought I could practise in the road after school.'

Linda was shocked. 'In the road? With boxwood wheels? You're joking!'

'I didn't know,' Giles said.

'You'll have to come down the Welfare Saturday morning,' she said. 'All the kids get down there. They chalk the floor and put barriers round. It's smashing.'

'I should feel silly, tumbling all over the place with people watching me.'

'Ten till eleven, beginners' hour,' she said. 'I'll

come with you and show you how to get on if you like.'

'If you would.'

She handed the skates back. 'And look,' she said. 'About last night. I'm sorry I made a mess of things.'

Giles shrugged his shoulders. 'I don't suppose it was a very good idea, anyway,' he said. 'I just got carried away arguing with old Mars Bar.'

'It was a good idea,' she said emphatically. 'Everybody thought so. I'll have a go at Martin later on, when he's in a good mood.'

Just then there was the sound of voices in argument; Mrs Maxwell and Martin. 'That's what mothers are for, isn't it?' Martin was saying angrily. 'You'd think I could find a clean shirt in my drawer when I want one. You go out to bingo and of course nothing's done.'

'If you change your shirts half a dozen times a day and then kick the dirty ones under the bed, what else can you expect?' shouted Mrs Maxwell.

'You just sit around all day. . . .' said Martin.

'Look who's talking? You haven't done a real stroke of work since you left school. . . .' came Mrs Maxwell's voice.

Linda ate her breakfast as if all this was no more than the sound of the wind and the rain. Between mouthfuls she said to Giles, 'I don't think I'd better try and get round Martin this morning, though.'

The argument went on for a few more minutes, then Mrs Maxwell burst into the room. 'That boy!' she muttered to herself. 'I'll do him an injury one of these days.'

Martin came in and banged himself down in a chair. He had a roll-top jersey on instead of a shirt. 'Well, where's my breakfast then?' he demanded loudly.

Mrs Maxwell snatched open the oven door and almost threw the plate of scrambled egg on toast at him. Martin seemed to think she was really going to, for he raised his hands quickly as if to defend himself. The edge of the plate hit his wrist and the plate spun in the air and spattered his face and hair with the egg.

For a moment there was a dreadful silence, Mrs Maxwell staring at her son and Martin staring back with a fixed expression on his face. Then he slowly raised one hand, scraped the egg off his forehead with one finger and thoughtfully put the finger into his mouth. 'Umm,' he said. 'Done just the way I like it; soft but not too squishy!'

Linda giggled, tried to stop and nearly choked herself. Mrs Maxwell started to laugh and leaned weakly back on the draining board for support. She missed the edge of the draining board and leaned instead on the handle of a saucepan full of cold water. The saucepan tipped up and poured water down the back of her legs.

Five minutes later all four of them were still laughing, though in an exhausted fashion, and trying rather feebly to help clear up the mess. Then they noticed the time and Linda and Giles had to rush to get to school on time.

'Your family really are a queer lot,' Giles gasped as they ran down the long, straight stretch of main road towards the school.

'How do you mean, queer?'

'Well, your mum, for instance. She goes mad at someone one minute, and the next she's forgotten all about it and is joking as if nothing's happened.'

'Oh, Mum! She does her top half a dozen times a day. You just have to get used to that. Dad's different, though. He hardly ever loses his temper. But when he does . . . you really want to watch out then; he means what he says.'

'Funny,' Giles said. 'I've never taken that much notice of grown-ups before. I suppose I must have thought they were all the same. But then I've never really had to live with them before.'

'Don't you like it?'

'I don't know,' said Giles. 'It takes some getting used to. Sometimes I like it; sometimes I don't.'

They were too puffed to talk any more after this and trotted along in silence. The road was quite empty – everybody seemed to have reached school.

When they turned the corner and could see the playground, they noticed that it was nearly empty with just the last two or three dozen children going in through the main doors. Sandra, however, was waiting for them at the gate.

'What have you two been up to?' she said. 'I thought you were never coming.'

'You needn't have waited,' said Linda.

'I didn't wait for you,' Sandra said. 'I was waiting for him – for Giles.'

'Well!' Linda exclaimed.

'Gribby asked me to give you this note,' Sandra went on, pulling an envelope out of her bag and handing it

77

to Giles. 'He lives next door to me, you know, and he said give it to you before we went in school for sure.'

'Thanks,' said Giles, taking the note and pushing his finger under the flap to open it.

A shout from the school door stopped him. The late-prefect was waving his book at them. 'What do you lot think you're up to, then?' he shouted.

They scurried for the door so as not to be listed as late and reached the hall breathless, but half a minute before Mr Norton entered to take assembly.

Giles had no opportunity to open the letter until almost the end of the first lesson when, having finished the maths set on the board, he was waiting for the master to come round and check his work. He slid the envelope out and opened it. The note was quite short, scrawled on a three-cornered piece of paper obviously torn off a grocery bag.

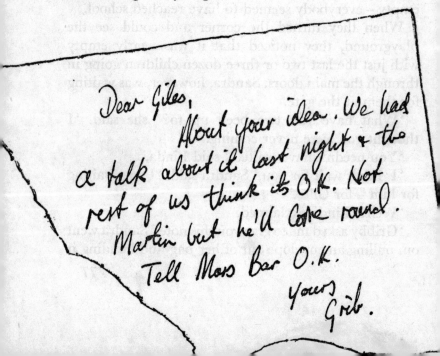

Dear Giles,
About your idea. We had a talk about it last night & the rest of us think its O.K. Not Martin but he'll come round.
Tell Mrs Bar O.K.
Yours
Grib.

Giles could hardly believe his eyes. But the letter seemed plain enough. All the same, he wrote on the bottom of the letter, 'Does he mean it or is it a joke?' and when he had the chance slipped the letter to Linda.

A few minutes later it came back to him. Linda had written at the very bottom. 'Good old Gribby! Better tell Mars Bar today and fix a date.'

He couldn't resist letting the rest of the class know, so while the maths master was at the far side of the room he wrote a note:

THE MINORS WILL BE COMING!
WATCH THIS SPACE
PASS IT ON

He set the note passing and watched the reactions as each member of the class read it and then turned to him with a grin or a wave of the hand or even an elaborate, silent cheer.

'Willis!' said the maths master, without raising his head from the work he was marking.

'Yes, sir?'

'Is your communication of a strictly mathematical nature?'

'I beg your pardon, sir?'

'You seem to be publishing some sort of information. In other words passing a note round the class. Of course, I may be wrong. . . .'

'No, sir. You're not wrong.'

'Will somebody be kind enough to read the note

aloud? Then we shall all know the good news at once and not be kept in suspense. It will also save time.'

There was a deathly silence, during which the note made a rapid passage across the class and landed back on Giles' desk.

'I think everybody's seen it now,' said Giles.

'Just to make certain,' said the maths master, 'read it to us, will you, Willis?'

Giles read out the first part of the note.

'How do you spell miners?'

'With an O, sir.'

The master showed immediate interest. He straightened up and positively beamed at Giles. 'Are they really?' he exclaimed. 'Now we were very divided on that question in the staff room. Mr Marshall was quite sure they wouldn't have the nerve to turn up. One or two teachers were against the whole thing. Mr Norton on the other hand was in favour of the idea, and also said it would be a pity to waste such an occasion on a simple music lesson. Yes, come to think of it, Willis, I think you'd better trot along to his room now and tell him the glad tidings. You have finished your maths, haven't you?'

'Yes, sir,' said Giles.

'Trot along then. And try and get back here before the bell goes; I'll be interested to hear what he says!'

Giles dived for the door. On his way up to Mr Norton's room he tried to puzzle out what the maths master had been saying. He hadn't imagined his little suggestion could be important enough to be discussed in the staff room. The light over the door was green, so he knocked and entered.

'Mr Barnard told me to come up, sir,' Giles said when Mr Norton looked up from his desk. 'He said you'd be interested. You see, sir, I suggested to Mr Marshall that it might be a good idea to ask the Minors to come down to the school and play for us. I mean, he's always talking about different sorts of music, so we ought to. . . .'

'Mr Marshall told me about it, Giles,' said Mr Norton. 'I take it you've some news?'

'I had a note from the drummer, sir, Gribby. He said they'd come. Gribby thinks it's a good idea.'

'So do I,' said Mr Norton. 'I think they should play in the hall to the whole school. Give them a proper audience.'

Giles hardly knew what to say. It was quite an honour, really. But would the Minors see it?

'Could we fix a day? Friday is always best. Friday afternoon.'

'I don't know,' Giles said. 'I'll ask Martin to-night.'

'Do that. And let me know tomorrow.'

'Yes, sir.' Giles still stood there.

'You look a bit bewildered, lad?'

'I am, a bit.'

'You've really started something, haven't you?'

'Yes,' said Giles, grinning nervously. 'And now I'm being carried along on it.'

9 Mr Maxwell's cough

Giles and Linda raced each other round the house to be first indoors. Linda won because she knew about swinging on the drain-pipe at the corner. Giles' speed along the path carried him out on to the lawn, while she gained a good three yards by checking and swinging close to the brickwork. She flung open the back door first into the kitchen.

'What do you think, Mum?' she shouted.

Mrs Maxwell came quickly through from the sitting-room. 'Try and be a bit quieter, love, will you?' she said.

Linda was too carried away with the news to be very observant. She swung round on Giles. 'You tell her,' she cried. 'I keep trying to push my great nose in, and it's your news really.'

Giles said, 'What is it, Mrs Maxwell? Is something the matter?' It seemed to him Mrs Maxwell looked different; she had a greyness round the eyes.

'Have you got a headache, Mum?' Linda said, suddenly conscious of the noise she was making. 'Oh, I'm sorry I came busting in like that. . . .'

'No, it's not me,' Mrs Maxwell said. 'It's Dad. They brought him back from the mine an hour ago.'

'Not an accident?' said Linda quickly.

'No. He had one of his coughing fits . . . I don't know yet how bad he is. . . .'

'I'm going up to see him,' said Linda, making for the bottom of the stairs.

'He may be asleep. Creep in, won't you?'

Linda went and Giles was left alone with Mrs Maxwell, who immediately went to the stove and filled a kettle in a dreamy sort of way. Giles did not know what to say. He would have liked to go upstairs to see Mr Maxwell but wasn't sure whether to ask or not. After all, it was Linda's father who was ill, not his.

Mrs Maxwell seemed to do something with her eyes to drag them back from the far distance she was gazing into. 'Oh, Giles,' she said. 'I expect you'd like a cup of tea, wouldn't you? And what was this news Linda was talking about? Has something exciting happened?'

'It's not important,' said Giles. 'Tell me about Mr Maxwell.'

'It's his chest,' she said. 'He had this trouble before, and we thought it was all done with. I don't like to think what might be the matter.'

'Linda told me how ill he was last time.'

'We had him at home nearly six months last time,' Mrs Maxwell said. 'It's so worrying. . . . Linda hasn't come down yet, so he must be awake. . . .' She didn't seem to know quite what she was doing. She wet the

83

tea and put the cosy on the pot and then began to fill the kettle again in an absent-minded way.

Linda came down, looking very serious. 'Dad's awake,' she said. 'Mum, do you think it's going to be like last time?'

'I'm sure I don't know. The doctor said he was to rest for a day or so and then they'd fetch him in to the hospital for X-rays and so on.'

'He says he'd like a cup of tea if you're making one.'

'Can I take it up?' said Giles quickly.

When he reached the bedroom door he felt a sudden nervousness. In some ways Mr Maxwell was still a stranger to him. Giles tapped on the door and went in.

Mr Maxwell was half-lying, half-sitting, three or four pillows behind his shoulders. He had a newspaper, but he hadn't been reading it. It was flat across his knees and he had his head tilted back slightly with his eyes closed. The shadows round his eyes were so dark they looked almost like bruises. He raised his eyelids with an effort, although they seemed thin and almost transparent; like greaseproof paper through which Giles could faintly see the colour of the eyes beneath.

'Did I wake you?' he asked. 'I'm sorry. . . .'

'No, I wasn't asleep . . . ah, tea!'

As he heaved himself higher in the bed he started to cough, stopped, and held himself quite still and rigid as if afraid of setting it off again. Gradually he relaxed and smiled wanly at Giles.

'Have to be careful,' he said and took the tea.

'Can I do anything?' said Giles. It's hard to think of things to say when someone is ill. You don't want to talk about illness in case it makes the person depressed, and yet there doesn't seem to be anything else important to talk about.

'There's a bit in the paper,' said Mr Maxwell. 'On the back page. About Manchester City's chances for the Cup this year. I always did fancy Manchester. Read me what it says.'

Giles was glad to do something. He took the paper and read out the piece Mr Maxwell had mentioned.

He went on to read other parts of the newspaper, any bits of news he thought might interest Mr Maxwell. After half an hour Mr Maxwell said:

'You'd better go down and get your tea. I think I'll have a little snooze now.'

'I didn't tire you?'

'Course not. Nice to have company.'

Giles went down and found they had been waiting tea for him. They ate it without talking, Mrs Maxwell staring at the cloth most of the time, her thoughts far away. Nothing whatever was said about the Minors playing at the school and how Mr Norton had shown an interest. It didn't seem important now.

However, later in the evening Gribby came round to ask Giles what had happened. Between them they fixed that the Minors would go down to the school the following Friday afternoon at three o'clock.

'I haven't said anything to Martin,' Giles said. 'You know how he is.'

Gribby laughed. 'Matter of fact he's quite keen,' he said. 'I think he just puts on a bit of an act.'

'He hardly talks to me,' Giles said. 'When I go up to bed and he's in the room, he just glares at me under his eyebrows. . . .'

'And you glare back,' said Gribby.

'I don't!'

'Not much! You ought to see yourself. Face like a wet Sunday afternoon most of the time. You're doing it now.'

Giles realized that his brows were in fact drawn together in a scowl. He hadn't thought about it before, but probably he did look like that most of the time. He pressed his eyebrows with his fingers.

'That's better,' said Gribby. 'You look quite human when you're not scowling.'

'I must try and remember,' Giles said. 'It's just nervousness, I suppose.'

'Anyway, I was saying. Martin's quite keen on this business at school, but he wouldn't say anything to you. He'd feel too embarrassed. Leave it to me, though. I'll tell him about Friday.'

After Gribby had left, Giles did his homework and then read for a while. The house was very quiet. No one turned the television or the radio on all evening; Mrs Maxwell spent most of the time upstairs with her husband. Giles had a feeling of being quite alone again, of being outside, a stranger. However concerned and worried he might feel about Mr Maxwell, still it was not his father but someone else's.

When he found he could no longer concentrate on his book, he shut it and went up to bed early. Martin was out, probably practising at the house of some other member of the group. Giles crept into bed, feeling depressed, and although he lay for a while staring at nothing in the darkness, he fell asleep before Martin came in.

When he woke next morning it was just getting light. The house was utterly silent, and that seemed queer until he remembered that early morning noises were usually made by Mr Maxwell getting himself off to work and that today of course he would not be going.

87

At that thought Giles came wide awake. He crept softly down the bed and over the end so as not to waken Martin, then took his clothes from the chair and carried them downstairs with him. He washed in the kitchen sink, dressed, and then with a feeling of excitement looked around to see what he could do.

For a start there was quite a lot of washing up from the night before. There always was; supper things, a few cups with traces of cocoa in the bottom, dirty saucepans. Some of the cups were on the floor in the sitting-room, under chairs where people had left them. Giles recovered all these before he ran the hot water. Then he washed up slowly and carefully, dried and put away.

What next? Tea! He put the kettle on. Five minutes later he carried up the tray with cups of tea.

Martin merely grunted and took his cup with his eyes still shut. Linda had her head under the covers; she kept it there and mumbled something about putting the cup on the chair. Not much of a reception, but Giles did not mind.

He hesitated outside Mr and Mrs Maxwell's door, not sure whether to walk in or not. In the end he tapped very lightly on the door and was relieved to hear Mrs Maxwell's voice telling him to come in. Both she and Mr Maxwell were awake.

'Tea!' said Mr Maxwell. 'You're a good lad!'

'I'll be getting up in a minute,' Mrs Maxwell said. 'Is it late?'

'No, not quite seven.'

'Good. No hurry then.'

Giles went back downstairs and, after having a cup of tea himself, looked round for any other jobs. He tried to think what Mr Maxwell usually did in the morning.

Milk bottles! He washed the empties and put them out on the step. He emptied the rubbish bin under the sink into the dustbin and put a fresh sheet of newspaper in the bottom. Then he noticed the fireplace in the sitting-room and he was still cleaning that out when Mrs Maxwell came down.

'You are busy,' she said.

Giles was amazed at how much there was to do if you really looked for jobs. He found plenty to keep him busy right up to school time. He resolved to do the same thing the next day.

On the following day Mr Maxwell was taken to hospital in the ambulance but was back in bed again before Giles and Linda returned from school. It was too early to expect any news. The X-ray department would let the Maxwells know in a few days what they thought of Mr Maxwell's condition.

So the week passed slowly. Giles kept to his resolution to get up early, and he tried to be as useful about the house as he could. He usually managed to spend some time each evening with Mr Maxwell, reading or talking to him, and the more time he spent with him the more he liked him.

On Thursday when he came home from school with Linda there was a car outside the door. His first thought was that it was the doctor or someone from the hospital.

89

'It's not the doctor's car,' Linda said. 'I've seen it before though.'

Suddenly Giles recognized it. 'Of course,' he said. 'It's Mr Judd's. I wonder what he wants?'

'Come over to see how you are, I expect,' said Linda. 'Did you think he'd just forget about you?'

'I wouldn't mind,' said Giles.

Mr Judd was sitting indoors drinking tea with Mrs Maxwell. He made an odd expression when Giles came in, Giles could not be sure what it meant. The talk did not seem to be about anything.

'I think I'll just pop upstairs and say hullo to Mr Maxwell,' Giles said. Mr Judd didn't seem to have come to see him.

'Just a minute, old chap,' said Mr Judd. 'I've got some news for you.' Then he looked at Mrs Maxwell as if waiting for her to speak.

'Well?' said Giles.

Mrs Maxwell said, 'Mr Judd's come to say he's got to take you back to the Home.'

'Why?' asked Giles, amazed. 'Have I done something wrong? Don't you want me here, then?'

'No, it's not that, Giles. Really,' said Mrs Maxwell. 'It's nothing to do with us . . . at least . . .'

'Does he have to go?' said Linda. 'We'd just about got used to each other. I can't see the point.'

'It's regulations,' said Mr Judd. 'We had a note from the hospital. I'm afraid you can't stay here, old chap.'

Giles felt that if Mr Judd called him 'old chap' again he would scream.

'We're not allowed to, you see. Until we know for sure what the trouble is. It's fairest for everybody. I mean, I don't suppose Mrs Maxwell wants the complication of having you here while she's worried about her husband. . . .'

'Oh, no,' cried Mrs Maxwell. 'Giles is no bother. Quite the opposite in fact. . . .'

'Even so,' said Mr Judd. 'As I've explained. Regulations have to be kept. So run upstairs, will you old chap, and pack your things. I'd like to leave in ten minutes or so.'

'Right now?' cried Giles. The whole thing was too sudden. He couldn't take it in properly.

'Yes,' said Mr Judd. 'Leaving in ten minutes.'

'Yes,' said Mr Judd. Hand...

10 First public appearance

On the way back in the car Mr Judd said, 'You
weren't with them long enough to get really attached
to them. That was a good thing, anyway.'

Giles did not answer.

Later Mr Judd said, 'You mustn't get disheartened,
you know. You've been a bit unlucky, that's all. Next
time we'll find you really good foster-parents, people
maybe who might want to adopt you. . . .'

Giles said fiercely, 'I don't want to go to any more
foster-parents. I've had enough of them. What's
wrong with being an orphan, anyway? Anyone would
think it was a crime or something.'

'No, of course not,' said Mr Judd. 'And perhaps it
would be better to leave it for a week or two. After all,
this might be a false alarm about Mr Maxwell, and
they might want you back again. Better to wait and
see.'

'I don't want to go back there again,' said Giles. 'I
didn't like any of them. And they don't care if they
never see me again.'

'Now you're just saying things you don't mean.'

92

'I do mean them; every word,' said Giles bitterly.

'Oh well . . .'

They drove the rest of the way in silence and when they arrived Giles carried his bag in and went up to see Matron.

'You are unlucky,' she said. 'Never mind, it's nice to see you again. You can have your old bed back again; no one's been using it.'

Giles found one of the boys he knew fairly well up in the dormitory. 'How did you get on?' the boy asked.

'You know what it's like.'

'Too true. Beastly. Still it makes a change from being here all the time.'

'I'm glad to be back,' Giles said. He felt that he meant it.

There was no question of his going on at Haleshangar school. Next morning he went off with the usual group of boys who went to the school nearest the Home. The teachers made various comments, none of them very funny, when they saw Giles in the class-room again. Giles put up with it all with a good grace. Then, as he was eating dinner in the big school hall, he suddenly remembered that it was Friday and that it was the day he had arranged with Mr Norton for the Minors to play to the school. And now he would not be there.

'Well, I don't care!' he said aloud.

'Don't care what?' said the boy next to him.

'Oh, nothing.'

All the same he found he did care. After dinner he

wandered down to the school gates and stood there looking down the road. He had no idea what made him stand there, but he had a sick, excited feeling in his tummy as if he was about to do something difficult for the first time, like dive off a very high board. The next moment he found himself walking briskly down the street away from the school, even breaking into a run when he reached the first corner. He knew it was a silly thing to do, but something made him and he could not stop.

After a while he found himself out on the road leading to Haleshangar. He waved an arm at a few passing cars and one of them stopped to pick him up.

'Where you going then?' the driver asked. 'Didn't you ought to be in school?'

'I'm trying to get back before the bell,' Giles said. 'I've been to the dentist's. . . .' The lie popped out before he'd thought.

'You might just make it,' said the driver.

He put Giles down at the corner of the road, and by sprinting to the gate he reached it just as the last of the children had entered the building. He went straight to his first lesson, which was maths, without having time to speak to anyone.

Linda was already in her desk. She looked at him with surprise, and then gave a wide, friendly grin. Giles sat down.

When the maths master checked the register he looked surprised too. 'Giles Willis?' he said. 'Why, I thought you'd left . . . oh, but of course, we've got this do in the hall, haven't we? I suppose you could hardly miss that.'

As no explanation seemed to be expected of him, Giles kept quiet. He settled down to work as usual. At the end of the lesson he seized the chance of asking Linda how Mr Maxwell was.

'They've taken him in to hospital,' she said. 'We're going in to see him tonight—at six o'clock.'

'Is he worse, then?'

'No. They said they wanted him in there for observation.'

And that was all there was time for. The next period was metalwork for the boys and domestic science for the girls. Giles was too busy working on a wrought-iron table lamp to have any time left for thinking of other things. As it happened he finished the lamp just before the end of the double period.

'You can take it home today if you want to,' said the master. 'I'd like it back for the exhibition of work at the end of the term, but I expect you'd like to show it to your mother now. It's a very nice piece of work. Good design, well carried out.'

When Giles had started on the lamp a couple of weeks before he had intended it as a present for Mrs Maxwell. Now he wasn't sure what to say. However, he said he'd take it. He thought he could always give it to Matron if no other idea came to him.

'Well, that's it,' the metalwork master said as the bell rang. 'Wash your hands and get down to the hall. We're all going to hear some music now—if you can call it music!'

Mr Norton had meant what he had said. The whole school were excused the last lesson of the afternoon in order to hear Martin's group. Giles noticed, as he took his place, that the whole of the staff were there too. They were laughing and talking among themselves as if trying to say that they had only come for a good laugh. Giles also noticed that Mr Norton had two youngish men with him that certainly weren't masters at the school. Maybe from the Education Office; inspectors or something, having a look to see what sort of thing Mr Norton got up to.

The excitement in the hall was of an odd sort. After all, most of the children either knew Martin or knew about him, and they certainly all knew about his group. On the other hand very few of them had heard the group play, as it had never appeared in public before.

There was not long to wait. Almost as soon as Mr Norton had entered, the door at the back of the school stage opened and the four boys entered. Their equipment was already set up at the back. Mr Norton stood in front of the stage and when the general noise had subsided, said:

'We're all very grateful to these four boys for coming down this afternoon. You know them, of course: they are all old boys of the school. I won't waste any more time with words, but leave it to . . . The Minors!'

Great applause and even a couple of screams from two rather hysterical girls in the third year. Mr Norton grinned and sat down.

Now for it, thought Giles. Suppose they're dreadful

96

and no one likes them! He touched the wooden back of his chair and then sat forward, eagerly concentrating on the group on the stage.

Giles need not have worried. The Minors were on top of their form.

They started off with a fast number with a tremendous beat, followed this with a ballad, then into a neat, quirky rhythmical piece with plenty of drums and bass guitar. Each item was greeted with ear-splitting applause. The group played on and on. It looked as if the audience would never let them stop.

After almost an hour Mr Norton jumped up on to the stage and held up his hand for silence. At first the school went on applauding and shouting for more and taking no notice of him, but gradually they sank back in their seats and waited to hear what he would say.

'I must say,' said Mr Norton, 'that when I arranged for these lads to play to the school I had no idea just how good they were. Now I'll tell you something Martin Maxwell himself ought to have told you, but was too modest to mention . . .'

There was a mild wave of laughter at this; it had never occurred to anyone that Martin was modest.

'No, I'm not joking. Martin's special form of gruffness is really his way of covering up a certain shyness. Well, he didn't tell you that more than half the numbers you've just heard were in fact written by him and Tom Gribbing . . .'

More wild cheers.

And so it went on. Mr Norton finally let the Minors play one more number and the school dismissed almost half an hour later than usual.

It was only when he was standing outside, watching the children streaming past him on their way home, that Giles suddenly realized with a shock that he ought not to be there at all. The other boys would be back at the Home by this time. They would have told the Matron that he had disappeared at dinner time and the Matron would most probably have told Mr Judd . . . or even the police. The best thing for him to do to avoid further trouble would be to hitch a ride back to town and report in as soon as possible.

He had just come to this conclusion when he found himself grabbed by the shoulders and turned round to find Gribby.

'Thanks a lot, kid,' Gribby was saying.

'Why me?' said Giles.

'Well, you started it, didn't you? It was your bright idea. And now look what's happened.'

'What has happened?'

'One of those chaps with the Head runs the Star Hall in Sungate. Mr Norton brought him round after, while we were packing up our kit, and he's booked us to play for the dancing on the first Saturday of each month for the next three months.'

'That's good,' said Giles.

'Good? It's fabulous! What's more, he's going to pay us!'

They talked for another minute or so, and then Gribby was just going when he caught sight of the table lamp Giles had been clutching ever since the end of metalwork lesson.

'That's pretty good,' he said. 'Did you make it for Mrs Maxwell? She'll like that, you know.'

After he'd gone Giles looked at the lamp as if seeing it for the first time. It was true he had made it in the first place as a present for Mrs Maxwell. Why not give

99

it to her, then? If he ran he could catch up with Linda and ask her to take it for him. He would be late at the Home now whatever happened; an extra ten minutes did not matter.

He broke into a run, back down the road towards the village, glancing quickly at everyone he passed. A lot of them grinned at him and shouted some sort of joke after him. He hadn't realized that so many people knew him. It gave him rather a good feeling inside to know that in Haleshangar at least he was somebody with a name, a proper person and not just 'one of those orphans from the Home'.

He caught up with Linda and a couple of her friends about a hundred yards from the Maxwells' house.

'Look, give this to your mum for me,' he exclaimed, thrusting the lamp into Linda's hands.

'Why me? Give it to her yourself,' she said, pushing it back at him. 'You're coming in, aren't you?'

'I can't really. I've got to get back. I ought not to be here at all.'

'I thought it was queer you turning up in maths like that.'

'Yes, well you take it.'

'Surely you can come in for a minute?'

'I ought not to . . .'

Linda grabbed his arm. 'Don't be so soft,' she said. 'Sandra, hang on to his other arm!' And before Giles could protest he found himself being rushed up the pathway of number 73.

11 Homing pigeon

'What a pleasant surprise,' said Mrs Maxwell.

'I shouldn't be here at all,' Giles said quickly.

'Not be here? Where else should you be then?'

'At the Home. They'll be wondering where I've got to. I didn't say . . . I just came . . .'

'Like a homing pigeon?' laughed Mrs Maxwell. 'Anyway, tea's ready, so you'll just have to stay and have tea with us.'

'I don't think I ought . . .' Giles found himself pulled both ways. He had the sensation of being wanted; of people wanting him to stay. Also the inside of the house, once he was through the front door, attacked him with its familiar smells and colours and shapes so as to seem almost like home. But at the same time he knew that every moment he stayed would give someone trouble.

'What utter nonsense,' Mrs Maxwell said. 'Now sit down and have something to eat. There's tinned salmon; I know you like that. And lettuce and water-cress and tomatoes . . . you can't walk out on that.'

Mrs Maxwell always had her own way when she

101

put her mind to it, and just now she seemed determined that Giles should stay to tea. Protesting and laughing and still protesting, Giles found himself sitting down with food piled on his plate and a knife and fork stuck in his hands.

'Now you keep an eye on him, Linda. I've got to rush next door for a minute . . .'

'A minute?' said Linda.

Mrs Maxwell laughed. 'I'm a dreadful gossip,' she said. 'I know. But not tonight. I want to hear all about the music this afternoon; how Martin got on and so forth.'

She dashed off and Giles seized the opportunity to plug in the table lamp and arrange it on a shelf so that the light fell on the chair that Mrs Maxwell usually sat in. He was only just in time, for Mrs Maxwell really was only gone a few minutes.

'All-time record,' said Linda.

'Be quiet, you,' said Mrs Maxwell, sinking back into her chair rather breathlessly. 'Now before you tell me about Martin. I didn't go next door; I went to the phone box and rang the Matron at your Home, Giles . . . here! Where did this lamp come from?'

'I made it at school for you.'

'Oh, Giles! That *was* nice of you. It's beautiful! What a lovely present!' She took the lamp down and admired it from every possible point of view. 'I'd no idea you were so clever . . .'

Giles was embarrassed but pleased. 'You were saying you phoned Matron?'

'Oh, yes, I told her you were quite safe and that

102

you were going to spend the evening here and I'd put you on the last bus. So that's fixed.'

'You *told* her?' Matron wasn't someone you told. If you were feeling brave you might ask her nicely.

'Yes,' said Mrs Maxwell. 'She seemed quite a nice old dear.'

Giles laughed.

'While I was on the phone I told her we wanted you back here as soon as it could be arranged. Now Mr Maxwell is in hospital, there's really no need for this silly regulation to be taken seriously. She said I was to come in and talk to her about it, so I'll go in tomorrow.'

Giles hardly knew what to say.

'Perhaps Giles doesn't want to come back,' said Linda, with a mouthful of lettuce. 'Probably glad to get away from us.'

Giles went absolutely scarlet with embarrassment as he said, or mumbled, 'I'd like to come back, if you can arrange it.'

'I'll arrange it,' said Mrs Maxwell. 'I shan't let them rest until I have. Don't you worry. Now! Tell me about Martin and the group. How was it?'

For the next half hour or so Linda and Giles told her what had happened in the hall, what Mr Norton had said, what Gribby had said afterwards. They were still more or less in the middle of it when Martin came in.

He bounced into the room in quite a new way; not at all the usual slouching, scowling Martin that they were used to. 'Wondered if I'd catch you,' he said to

103

Giles. 'Gribby said you were around. You heard the show?'

'I certainly did,' said Giles. 'Showed old Mars Bar a thing or two. It was tremendous. But you heard the noise the kids made, so you know what they all thought.'

'First time we've played to a crowd,' said Martin. 'A bit frightening to tell you the truth. My fingers felt like boiled sausages for the first couple of numbers. Well, you did us a bit of good with your argument with Mars Bar.' He was suddenly taken with an awkward cough and added in an offhand way, 'Many thanks anyway.'

Some time later, sitting in the bus, Giles felt warm and happy without really knowing why. He wondered why he liked being in the Maxwell's house. After all, they were an odd family, not at all easy to get on with. Linda was still her bossy self, and you never knew what mood Mrs Maxwell was going to be in next. He could not understand why he liked them. And what was even odder, they seemed to like him.

'You're a naughty boy,' Matron said.

Giles didn't really mind being told off.

'You shouldn't have gone in the first place,' Matron said.

Giles started to grin and quickly changed it into what he hoped was a serious expression.

'Mr Judd said you didn't even like that family. He said you didn't want anything more to do with them. We've been trying to find you somewhere else.'

'They're quite nice really,' Giles said. 'But it isn't

104

that. The thing is I've got sort of mixed up with them. I mean, now Mr Maxwell's in hospital, well, who's going to get the morning tea, and do the extra washing up, and the fires? Well, there are a lot of little jobs and someone has to do them.'

Matron tried to prevent herself smiling at this. 'Now look,' she said in a serious voice. 'It would be a lot better if you forgot about the Maxwells. The chances of your going back to them are very small indeed. You'll just be disappointed if you keep thinking about it.'

'But why?'

'I suppose you know why Mr Maxwell is in hospital?'

'Not really.'

'They think it's an infection of the lung. Tuberculosis it's called. And if they're right it will mean Mr Maxwell may well go off to a sanitorium for months. In which case the family will have very little money coming in.'

'All the more reason why I should go to them. It would help,' said Giles.

'I'm afraid that's not the way the authorities look at it. We like to make absolutely certain that our children will be well cared for. And if we can't be sure . . .'

'Well, that's not fair!'

'Perhaps not, but there it is. Now run along to bed and think over what I've said.'

Giles climbed up to the dormitory feeling very depressed, and it was quite some time before he could get to sleep. He kept thinking of Mr Maxwell being ill, of the family getting poorer . . . if only he could do something.

The following day was Saturday. When Giles woke up he remembered that Mrs Maxwell was coming in to talk to Matron, and because of this he spent the whole morning hanging about the Home. He would not even join the boys in their weekly game of football on the recreation ground, although this was something he usually looked forward to eagerly.

He spent hours just wandering around the building getting in people's way and keeping a sharp look-out from the upstairs windows. There was a gravel drive up to the house, and it was easy to see when someone was approaching the front door.

About eleven his watch was rewarded; he saw Mrs Maxwell, looking very smart and young and pretty, walking towards the front door. Giles waved, but she did not look up, so he raced downstairs and reached the hall just in time to open the front door to her.

'Why, Giles?' she said. 'I came to see Matron.'

'I know,' said Giles. 'I'll take you to her. How is Mr Maxwell?'

'No news yet. But they're moving him to the Branwell Chest Hospital on Monday. Maybe they'll sort it all out.'

'Is that good news or bad?'

'Neither so far. We're just keeping our fingers crossed.'

'Ah, Mrs Maxwell, isn't it? I've been expecting you!' This was Matron who had crossed the hall and

106

was smiling at Mrs Maxwell. 'All right, Giles. Run along now.'

Giles went slowly back upstairs, but stopped when Mrs Maxwell and Matron went into Matron's room. Then he came back a little way and sat down on the stairs where he could peer through the banisters and see Matron's door.

About half an hour later the door opened again and Mrs Maxwell came out. By this time one of the staff was waiting at the door to speak with Matron, so she did not show Mrs Maxwell to the door but went back into her room. Giles thanked his stars and slid down the stairs quickly.

'Well?' he said.

'Oh, you did give me a shock. Well what?'

'What did Matron say?'

Mrs Maxwell smiled and shrugged her shoulders. 'I didn't get anywhere,' she said. 'Wait and see, that's all.'

'You mean I can't come back to you?'

'She said you could come over once a week for a visit, but that was all. Otherwise we've got to wait for news from the hospital.'

'When can I come over then?'

'Tomorrow?'

'Yes, please.'

In this way began a time of waiting that seemed to Giles to go on for ever. He went over to see the Maxwells on the following day, and as the weather was springlike and mild, they all went for a walk down towards the farm where Giles had seen the gulls following the plough on his first day. But after that followed a whole week with no news of any sort. Giles went to school and came back, did his homework, went to bed and then went to school again.

The following weekend he spent another day at Haleshangar. The first thing he noticed was that the television set had disappeared.

'Is it broken or something?'

'We couldn't keep up the payments,' Linda said. 'The programmes were horrible anyway. We don't really care.'

Giles realized that the Maxwells were getting short of money. Of course, while Mr Maxwell was in hospital he was not getting paid. Matron had said something about it. Giles felt quite uncomfortable when he saw there was his favourite tinned salmon for tea.

Another empty week followed, the only bright spot of which was a letter from Linda which arrived on Thursday morning.

Dear Giles,

Mum says will you come over Sunday this weekend as we are all going up to see Dad on the Saturday.

What about this for news though? When the Minors were playing at the Star Hall last time a man came up and asked Martin if he would like to make a record of two of the tunes he and Gribby wrote. It's only a small company, the record people, I mean. No one important like any of the big names. Still, it's something.

> *See you Sunday then,*
> *Linda.*

That Saturday was the longest day Giles could ever remember. Why hadn't they asked him to go up to see Mr Maxwell with them? He would have liked to go. Now he had this great, dead day in front of him, and nothing he wanted to do.

'Are you sure you're not sickening for something?' one of the staff said suspiciously when she found him lying on his bed staring at the ceiling. 'Shall I ask Matron to give you something or other?'

Giles shook his head. 'I'm all right,' he said and got off the bed. He pretended to be sorting some things out in his cupboard for a while. It seemed a year to lunch-time, two more years to tea-time, and then there was still the evening to go. Giles decided he could bear it no longer. He would have a hot bath and go to bed

109

early. If he could get to sleep that would be one way of making the time pass more quickly.

He was in bed by half past six, but although the bath had made him drowsy he could not get off to sleep. He was just beginning to drowse off some time just after eight, when one of the boys came and stood by his bed.

'Are you asleep?' he said.

'Yes,' said Giles, trying not to move his mouth too much or open his eyes in case he should wake right up again.

'Oh, I'll tell them, then,' said the boy and walked away.

'Tell who?' said Giles, sleepily.

'Some people come to see you.'

'I don't know any people,' mumbled Giles and pulled the covers higher.

'Called Maxfield, or Maxstead or something. Four of them.'

Giles sat bolt upright, coming awake as if he'd been shot from a gun.

'Maxwell?'

'Could be.'

'Not four though.'

'I can count that far,' said the boy. 'Man and a woman, a tough-looking chap about eighteen and a girl . . . here! You can't go down there in your pyjamas!'

'Want to try and stop me?' cried Giles, pushing him out of the way.

12 Giles had better be told

There was no mistake. It was indeed Mr Maxwell, looking very well and extremely pleased with himself, standing in the middle of his family, who all looked as if they had just won some stupendous prize or been voted the best family of the year. Giles' first feeling on seeing them all so pleased and close together was one of envy, but this only lasted a fraction of a second, less than the time it took to run down one stair, and then it was swept away in a great feeling of pleasure for them and delight at seeing Mr Maxwell, obviously better again.

'We came as quickly as we could,' said Mr Maxwell. 'But we didn't expect to find you in bed so early. Are you ill or something?'

'No,' cried Giles. 'Fed up, that's all. But I'm not any longer. Are you really better?'

'It was a false alarm, luckily,' said Mr Maxwell. 'They gave me a few days of this modern treatment just to make sure and to get rid of this cough, and then they threw me out. I feel a bit of a fraud, worrying you all.'

111

As he was talking Linda was shaking her father's arm. 'Dad!' she cried. 'That's not what we came for. Tell him! Don't keep on going round and round in circles. Tell him!'

'Tell me what?' asked Giles suspiciously.

Mr Maxwell refused to be hurried. 'We could have got here earlier,' he said, 'but we had a few other calls to make first.'

'Oh, Dad!' exclaimed Linda impatiently.

'Yes,' said Mr Maxwell. 'Quite a lot of calls actually. We've been to all the important people who seem to be concerned in the future happiness of Giles Willis and we've shown them papers from the hospital and documents from doctors and we've finally managed to fix it.'

'Fix what?' said Giles as Mr Maxwell seemed to have stopped there.

Linda could stand it no longer. 'You can come back with us, you chump.'

'Right now?'

'Yes, right now. This very moment.'

Giles could hardly believe it. The way he widened his eyes and stared at them made them burst out laughing. 'Well, what are we waiting for?' he said at last.

Mrs Maxwell laughed. 'At the moment,' she said, 'we're waiting for you to put some proper clothes on!'

Giles looked down at himself. He had forgotten by this time that he was still in pyjamas. 'I'll be two minutes,' he said and fled up the stairs.

It took longer than two minutes in fact. He had to

pack his bag and then there was a little interview with Matron, but within half an hour they were all on the bus to Haleshangar, and within an hour they were all indoors at number 73, sitting down to a fish and chip supper.

This had been Martin's idea. Mrs Maxwell looked doubtful when he suggested it, and put her hand in her handbag as if she doubted whether she could afford to pay for it.

'My treat,' said Martin. 'Don't forget I'm a working lad now.'

As he dashed off to get the fish and chips from the shop round the corner, Giles quietly asked Linda what he had meant.

'He gets paid pretty well from the Star,' she said. 'And they've had some other jobs from that. But he's been giving lessons in the guitar at five shillings an hour to some of the kids in Haleshangar.'

Mrs Maxwell overheard this. 'Martin's been giving me money,' she said. 'I don't know how we should have managed while Dad was in hospital otherwise.'

Martin burst in with the steaming packages while they were talking. 'Quick, while it's hot!' he said, opening the paper on the table and flicking a couple of chips into his mouth.

'Martin!' cried Mrs Maxwell. 'Don't be such a barbarian. I've got some plates warming in the oven!'

And then they all sat down to a hilarious meal.

Giles settled back into life at Haleshangar as if he had never been away. Everything was so familiar and natural, he sometimes had the odd feeling that he had

113

been dreaming during the months and even years that had gone before. The time in the Home, the shuttling backwards and forwards between different foster-parents, these times began to go misty and vague in his mind. An unpleasant dream, but a dream all the same. It was as if he had never had any other proper home but this one.

When he had been back with them another week, Mr and Mrs Maxwell suggested that it would be a lot easier if he called them Mum and Dad instead of the long-winded Mr Maxwell and Mrs Maxwell. Giles found it awkward for a few days, but his tongue soon got used to it and in fact found that it was a lot more natural and easy.

During that week Martin delivered a bombshell. 'Look,' he said one evening when he and Giles were just getting ready for bed, 'the Minors have got this recording session tomorrow. Do you think you could take the day off school?'

'Why me?' said Giles.

Martin threw his socks across the room in his usual way. 'Oh,' he said carelessly, 'you could hold the microphone or something.'

Giles laughed. 'You don't really need me, though.'

'Of course, if you don't want to come . . .' said Martin.

'I'd like to come, naturally.'

'Well then. That's fixed then.' Martin hopped into bed and started reading the musical weekly that gave details of new songs and records. 'We just had the queer idea you'd bring us luck if you came,' he added.

'Don't turn the light out just yet . . . and don't jump on my ankle when you get in bed, like you did last night.'

Giles took quite a long time to get to sleep that night. He was thinking of the next day, excited at the idea of going up to London with the Minors. He was also particularly pleased that the group should want him to go with them.

Every single incident of that day stayed in Giles' memory for years after. It wasn't just the strange happenings in the recording studio itself—which turned out to be a disused film studio in what was more like a great aircraft hangar than a proper building. Every single item of the journey seemed somehow special; the Underground stations in London, the taxi they took, the Indian restaurant they had lunch at, the waiters who served it, the odd food, the voices behind the partition speaking softly to each other in a strange language, everything.

On the train home that evening, Giles slept for a while, worn out by all that had happened. He woke up to find himself in yet another taxi which the boys had hired for the last bit of the journey out to Haleshangar. And there, to end the day, Mrs Maxwell made them all go in and eat a huge savoury omelette and an immense bowl of trifle and tell the family exactly what had happened.

The rest of the week fell rather flat. As Martin said, it might be months before they actually brought the record out; it wasn't something that just happened in a day. Giles had imagined they would be able to bring the finished record away with them after the recording session, so he was very disappointed. And when no news came during the next fortnight, he simply pushed it all away into the back of his mind and forgot it.

Meanwhile life went on pretty well as usual. Mr Maxwell went back to work; the television appeared again in its usual corner; the Minors were allowed to practise as much as they liked in Martin and Giles' bedroom, and even the neighbours, who had heard of the record, did not make any fuss.

Giles found that Martin was much easier to get on with. He was still moody and bad-tempered at times, but these fits never lasted long nowadays. He didn't slouch around in the old way either. Even though Mr Maxwell was back at work, Martin went on giving his mother money every week—in fact he seemed pleased to do so—as if he wanted to prove that he could earn a living just as well as anyone else, even though he wasn't down the mine hacking out coal.

The days and the weeks passed. Mr Judd called now and then, asked Giles how he was, had a cup of tea with Mr and Mrs Maxwell, and then went off again. If it hadn't been for these visits, Giles would by now have forgotten all about the Home and his old life.

One day, just after Mr Judd had gone, Giles said, 'Why does he keep coming like that?'

'To see we're not beating you,' said Mr Maxwell, with a grin.

'No, but really?'

116

'Well, you're still their responsibility, you see. They have to make sure you're happy.'

'I wish I wasn't.'

'Wasn't what?'

'Wasn't still their responsibility. Why can't they just forget about me and leave me here with you?'

'You might not want to stay. People change their minds.'

'I shan't ever change mine,' said Giles.

Mrs Maxwell said, 'What about when I do my nut at you sometimes? Like the other day when I found three dirty shirts stuffed down behind your bed?'

Giles thought for a minute. 'It may sound daft,' he said, 'but I *like* it when you tell me off. Being told off is sort of part of being in a family.'

He noticed Mr and Mrs Maxwell exchanging queer glances and wondered what it was about. Had he said something bad?

'What about those blue and pink forms Mr Judd brought last time?' he said. 'Do you have to keep filling them in just to say I'm happy and would like to stay here for ever?'

Again Mr and Mrs Maxwell looked at each other. 'Do you think we should tell him?' Mrs Maxwell said.

'We decided not to just yet.'

'I know, but . . .'

Giles felt a nasty empty feeling inside him. He must have done something wrong. They were going to send him back to the Home and they hadn't liked to tell him. Of course, now that Mr Maxwell was well and

117

Martin was making money, they didn't need the
extra money from the Home. He felt as if the whole of
his inside was turning to lukewarm water. At the same
time saliva started running over his tongue, and he
was almost sure he was going to be sick. He managed
to swallow hard.

'I think you'd better tell me,' he said in a faint,
choked voice.

Mrs Maxwell looked at her husband. 'Go on, then!'
she said.

Mr Maxwell looked at his shoes. He scratched at a
little patch of mud on the knee of his trousers. 'A few
days ago,' he said slowly, 'we filled in some forms about
you and sent them off. We didn't want to say anything
until the official part was over and done with. Just in
case anything went wrong . . .'

'Forms?' said Giles. 'To the Home?'

'Well, one for the Home. And some others for . . .'

'You're going to send me back, aren't you?'

There was a shocked silence as they both stared at
him.

'Back?' said Mrs Maxwell. 'Do you want to go
back? I thought you just said . . .'

'Of course I don't want to. But it's obvious, isn't it?
I mean, you don't need . . .' Giles found he couldn't
go on because something got in the way of the words.

Mrs Maxwell jumped up and came over to him.
She bent down and put her hand over both his. 'Oh,
Giles!' she exclaimed. 'Not back. Not back to the
Home. Don't you understand? We've been applying
for permission to adopt you.'

118

It took a long time for the words to drop into the right places in Giles' head. When he looked up again he felt quite different. As if he was filled with bubbles almost. He breathed out a long sigh. 'Oh,' he said. 'That's all right, then.'

Mrs Maxwell squeezed his hands, and when he looked at her face it struck him that her eyes looked odd; as if she was going to cry at any moment.

'Look,' he said, 'I can't lend you a handkerchief. I couldn't find a clean one this morning. I think you might find a pile of dirty ones behind the chest of drawers though . . .'

Mrs Maxwell made a queer noise and rushed out of the room.

'Do you think I've made her cross?' Giles asked Mr Maxwell.

'I don't think so. You had us on edge for a bit, when we thought we might have done the wrong thing. But it's all right now.'

Mrs Maxwell came back a few minutes later, smiling and blowing her nose on one of Mr Maxwell's handkerchiefs to show that everything was all right. She had just sat down again when the back door crashed open like an explosion and Martin and Linda rushed into the room.

'You haven't even got it on!' shouted Martin furiously.

'Really, Martin . . .'

Martin leapt at the television set and turned it on.

'We don't want the television on now,' Mrs Maxwell said. 'We've just been talking to Giles about . . .'

'Listen!' cried Linda and pointed at the screen as if something absolutely monstrous was going to appear. Instead it was just the well-known face of a popular disc jockey.

'Oh, really . . .' objected Mrs Maxwell. 'You can have this any time . . .'

'. . . and to end with,' the disc jockey was saying, 'we're going to play you a brand-new release from a brand-new group. To my ear it's got a new sound and I think the kids are going to like it. It probably won't reach the top ten, but it's my bet it'll climb to eighteen or nineteen in the charts . . . Here it is . . . "Break it to her gently" with the Minors.'

As the music began to play there was a thumping on the front door. 'Next door, to tell us,' said Mrs Maxwell and ran to let them in.

'Half Haleshangar'll be round,' said Mr Maxwell.

Martin waved his hands conducting it, listening to his own voice pouring out of the loud-speaker.

'All in one day,' said Giles. 'I think I shall be sick after all.'

Linda said, 'Have they told you about the adoption papers? Fabulous, isn't it?'

'Which? The adoption or the music?'

'Both,' she said. 'Do you have to be sick?'

'I don't think I've got time,' Giles said. 'There's too much to think of.'

Linda grinned. 'I told Sandra we were related,' she said. 'I must have known this was coming all the time.'